The Forgotten Five

Levelling Up Together

BOOK 1

ANKA B. TROITSKY

Copyright © 2025 Anka B. Troitsky
Published in the UK by Greystone Consultancy LTD
ISBN: 978-1-0683590-0-2

To all games and players, friends, lovers and dreamers

I am grateful to my editor, Andrew Hodges, The Narrative Craft.

Hello, precious reader.

I am your storyteller tonight.

Some fantasy campaigns never make it to the table, the map, the console, or even the game itself.

They disobey me. They break free after a few chapters and begin lives of their own.

This is one of those stories.

If you are looking for a game to play, you may need another book.

But if you wish to visit my Zemeland, walk its roads, meet its heroes, listen to the songs of everybody's favourite Digram Oldbook and breathe... no, step away from Fluffy first. Down, boy!... and breathe the air of adventures you missed, then come with me.

The story is about to begin.

I have never been very good at straight lines myself. I prefer going deep. Deeper than magic. Deeper than any sword can cut.

I hope you are ready.

- The Author

Contents

Epigraph

"Draw out of me what I really want -
surely, I cannot wish for anything wicked!"

Strugatsky's Brothers. ***Roadside Picnic***

1: Walking and Talking Tree

Oh, look! Some funny footprints! Let's examine them. I sense that this is the beginning of my story, right here.

Four sets of footprints on the damp ground that seem to belong to four different creatures, although only three walkers are wearing shoes. Most sets are deep enough to suggest they carry a significantly heavy load. One walker clearly limps slightly and wears ordinary human riding boots with heels and stirrups. Another has boots with broad soles that leave large, deep prints. The distance between these prints indicates short legs and a small but heavy posterior. The third also appears to carry a burden, but the prints suggest their owner hardly touches the ground. Their shoe soles are narrow and elegantly shaped. The last footprints are barefoot, with broad feet and spread-out toes, but the distance between the prints is small, as if a child has walked there.

All four walkers hike for hours. They stop and rest a few times, creating areas of well-stomped ground, but not for long. If we follow them, we might find where they stop to spend the night.

The sky grows darker, but we can still see the edge of the old forest and the campfire. It must be them. Let's move closer. Two couples are wrapped in blankets and animal hides on opposite sides of a pile of gleaming embers. On the left, two tall people sleep in a loving embrace. All we can see is the night breeze occasionally lifting their strands of hair — one blond, the other brunette. Both have long hair, partially braided and modestly decorated with gems, pearls, silver beads and feathers.

At first, the other couple looks like two children holding each other in their sleep. Yet, on closer inspection, their weathered faces and broad shoulders tell a different story, especially the stern one's face. The bare feet of the smaller person stick out of the blanket. But it is not the cold air that wakes this little guy. He sits up and listens intently, his brown curly locks falling over his eyes.

There is no way they can hear or see us, but something alarms the traveller. He gently leans over his partner and calls out, "Beryl?"

But a heavy snore is his only answer.

A glance at his friends on the other side of the camp calms him a little. Then the noise comes again. It is unclear where it comes from, and at first, it sounds like a simple creak of one branch against another in the wind, only much lower and almost explicit, like a single word. The meaning of that word is unknown.

The traveller gets up and adds some wood to the fire.

A few dark birds wake and rise above the distant trees. The moon emerges from the clouds, and the traveller spots a young tree a few paces away. Since it was his duty to collect firewood that evening, he is sure he found every dry twig and piled up every dead branch in this area. He remembers his friend's advice not to approach the forest at this hour and not to dare to break the branches of living trees. Despite that advice, if he had spotted this tree so close to the camp, he would have at least thought about cutting it down. Perhaps he got distracted and missed it somehow.

The traveller turns away from the forest and looks back at the meadow, scanning the tall grass for movement. Everything looks in order. He turns back to the woods and almost jumps.

The young tree is practically in front of him, just a few steps away.

"What the ..." he starts but becomes completely speechless when he sees a pair of eyes looking at him. They are close to each other because the top part of the tree trunk is no wider than his leg. They look like a couple of identical emeralds embroidered into the thin bark. A small hollow opens beneath the eyes; from it, a black swallow flutters out and flies away. The traveller hears the same soft sound of a creaking branch. This time, it is unmistakable.

"Name?"

It is said so quietly that the small traveller lowers his voice in response, careful not to wake his friends.

"What? My name? Heh ... My name is Digram. Digram Oldbook."

He waits for a whole minute before he hears the response.

"Kol . . . son of . . . Dryn."

Digram eyes the walking tree suspiciously but decides to keep the conversation friendly.

"Nice to meet you, Kol. What can I do for you?"

"Listen. Must . . . listen. I have . . . much . . . to tell you . . . Digram . . . Old . . . Book."

"Deep inside, I was afraid you'd say that."

The leaves, too green for the late summer, rustle frantically though there's no strong wind.

"Listen!"

"Okay . . . Okay. Keep your bark on. Go ahead. I love a good story."

"My father . . . told me . . . to warn you . . ."

Digram listens intently. At first, he stands in front of the young tree. Then, he sits down on a flat rock nearby. After a moment, he begins to circle Kol slowly, twirling a long grass stem in his hands and occasionally striking off the heads of plantains growing nearby. The night slips away unnoticed, and the dawn paints the sky in brilliant pinks and blues.

Digram interrupts the tree's tale and asks, "Do you mind carrying on while I start making breakfast for my friends?"

He tosses a few more twigs onto the fire and retrieves ham and eggs from his backpack. The smell of coffee and an omelette rouses the dwarf first.

Kol pauses politely — he's nearly finished anyway.

"Morning, love," Digram says as Beryl sits up, her gaze fixed on the tree.

"Diggie, what's going on?"

"Let me introduce you two. This lady, who hasn't had time yet for her morning shave, is my wife, Beryl, from the Palecliffs clan. Beryl, this is Kol, son of Dryn. He's here to help us with our quest. Apparently, he doesn't quite fit in with his family. They say he talks too fast."

"I bet he does," Beryl replies drily. Then, louder, she barks, "Hey, lovebirds! Wake up! We missed something here."

The elven man stirs immediately, kicking off the blanket. He checks his bow first, then surveys the situation. Satisfied there's no immediate threat, he places a hand on the shoulder of the black-haired woman beside him and shakes her gently. The human woman, with much darker skin and broad eyebrows, opens her beautiful eyes and blinks several times at the young tree.

"Kol, these are my friends and travelling companions, Lord Vaelior and Lady Minelira. They need to hear what you told me even more than I do," Digram says, pouring coffee into four brown cups. "He's brought us an important message from Dryn, his father — a warning I've been forced to listen to for most of the night."

"Ah, yes, a walking tree!" says the Elven Lord Vaelior with interest. "Kol? I knew Dryn, your father, when he was about your age. He's not an ancient one, is he?"

"No," Kol replies, his voice lilting like a spring breeze, unsure of its direction.

Vaelior hands a cup to Lady Minelira. "I've heard tales of Dryn's experiments. Though I suspect he's a bit biased, being a tree and all. Did you know, my love, he once tried to convince a band of orcs to switch to a vegetarian diet?"

Minelira accepts the cup with a raised eyebrow. "Orcs? Vegetarians? That's ambitious."

"Ambitious? Indeed!" Vaelior's blue eyes shine with amusement. "But it didn't go well. They found it distasteful — literally!"

"Fascinating," Beryl mutters, rubbing sleep from her eyes. "But could your new friend get to the warning? We don't have all day, you know."

"It is done," says the rustling voice. Kol's emerald eyes vanish, sinking into the bark. The hollow closes as the swallow flutters back inside, and without turning, the tree moves towards the forest at least five times faster than a large snail.

The elf, the dwarf and the human all begin eating their portions of the omelette, their gazes fixed on the halfling.

"Looks like it is down to me now," says Digram, his tone a mixture of resignation and enthusiasm. "Okay. Kol says we will die if we move through the forest. It is full of traps and enchanted trees that will crush us like bugs as soon as we enter. There are also giant spiders and flesh-eating fungi. Going around it is also not an option, as the forest spreads for weeks of walking in both directions. We don't have supplies for such a journey. But he does not suggest we should go back either. There is a way. We can go underground into the tunnels of the stone moles. We will need our weapons, and we will need light."

Digram finishes his coffee and pours some more from the pot.

"Go on," says Beryl, her brow furrowing as she contemplates their options.

"This is it," Digram says, leaning forwards. "If you want details, you can chase Kol and ask him yourself, my priceless gem."

Beryl turns to look at Kol, who is still running just behind her back as fast as he can.

"I thought you said you were listening all night."

"And I did," Digram replies, shrugging.

"Right. I see. So let's break it down: a haunted forest, murderous fungi and friendly neighbourhood spiders. I was looking forward to it, but I think the underground is more appealing to my nature," Beryl says. "Any chance you're leaving out the part about how we get into these tunnels?"

"Ah, well, that's the kicker!" Digram grins almost conspiratorially. "Kol mentions the entrance is hidden beneath a mossy rock shaped like a ... well, a rather unfortunate-looking mushroom."

"Charming," Minelira says. "And how do we find this rock? Surely it won't just wave and say, 'Here I am, come enter my dark and dank lair!'"

"No, no, that would be too easy!" Digram says as though it is the most logical thing in the world. "The trick is to find the right glade, the one where the birds seem to chat to each other in a language you can almost understand — about the good old days when the world was much less complicated."

Vaelior raises an eyebrow. "And how do we know when we find this glade? Will it be marked with a signpost saying 'Welcome to the Spooky Fungi Forest: Enter at Your Own Risk'?"

"Close enough!" Digram chuckles. "You'll know it when you see it. The trees will have a peculiar twist to their trunks as if they've been engaged in an animated debate about the best way to grow."

"And if those trees or spiders attack us?" Beryl asks, uncrossing her arms. "I'd rather not be caught off guard. Pass me those cups and plates, Diggie. I will wash them in the stream."

"Fear not, my friends," Digram replies, lifting his fist full of spoons and forks, "for I have a plan! We'll distract them with a bit of music. This morning, I shall write a new song that will charm even the most cantankerous entities. If nothing else, it should at least make them stop and wonder, 'What on Mid-Earth is that noise?'"

Minelira sniffs. "You think a song will save us from the very real danger lurking in those woods?"

"Of course!" Digram exclaims as if it is the most obvious thing in the world. "Music soothes the wood spirits, or at least distracts them long enough for us to escape."

Vaelior cannot help but laugh. "Well, if we're doomed, at least we'll go down singing!"

"Exactly!" Digram says, his face brightening. "Now, let's gather our supplies and find this glade. Adventure awaits!"

Of course, everyone knows Digram is only joking, and they all play along. The change of plans isn't a laughing matter. Nevertheless, the group begins to pack their belongings, smirks and banter filling the air as they ready themselves for the strange and uncertain journey ahead. After all, in a world full of magic, mayhem and just the right amount of mischief, what could possibly go wrong?

2: Song for the Road

Ah yes, dear reader, the stone moles. A creature of such peculiarity that even nature itself might take a moment to say, "Well, that's a bit much, isn't it?" before hastily stuffing them underground to be forgotten about. If you will, imagine something caught halfway between a rodent and an arachnid, as though evolution got distracted mid-process and never quite got around to finishing the job.

These delightful horrors are blind. Because they naturally live underground and have no use for eyes when they can rely on far more unsettling methods of locating their next meal. Only their claws, long and spindly like something a particularly nasty hedge would produce, ever breach the surface. These claws follow a simple but effective philosophy: grab anything that dares tread above. No discrimination, mind you; biped, quadruped, octoped (if that's even a thing), all are welcome on the menu. They get snatched and dragged into the labyrinthine depths below, where, I imagine, the moles are probably rather pleased with themselves.

Now, if you are lucky — and by "lucky" I mean "have the audacity of a person who plays cards with Fate and wins" — you might only lose a limb. History scrolls record a few such survivors. They emerge pale, shaken and with a newfound appreciation for sturdy footwear, telling tales of creatures with drill-like snouts and mouths that can only be described as, how to put this delicately?, a dental horror show. These creatures, it seems, prefer to crush their victims first and chew later. Even the most fearsome denizens of the forest, giant spiders and the like, seem positively cuddly after you hear about these creatures. At least spiders have the decency to poison their food before consuming it.

But here's the odd thing: no one has seen a stone mole in over a hundred years. Zemeland, once their favourite hunting area, remain curiously quiet. No tremors, unfortunate accidents at the local watering holes, or missing travellers. It's as if they've vanished, or worse, have gone elsewhere. So, you might be thinking, "Ah, excellent! Surely they're gone for good if they've not been seen in a century?" Well, my dear reader, I wouldn't count on it. Creatures like that, ones with a propensity for burrowing and lurking, have a habit of turning up when least expected.

And if I may offer one small piece of advice: should you ever find yourself in the

Zemeland, walking along an old migration path, and you notice the ground beneath your feet feels too thin — well, you might want to tread lightly. Or better yet, take up flying, just in case.

Now, let's go back to our heroes. Oh no, we just missed them! They are gone! The camp is empty, and the last few blackened chunks of what was once a campfire no longer smoulder.

The human, the elf, the dwarf and the halfling must have left quite a while ago. But look ahead, where four figures tread softly towards the forest — well, three of them tread softly; the fourth, the halfling, belts out a tune loud enough to wake the local owl from its morning nap (and we all know how owls feel about that sort of thing).

As Digram's cheerful voice rings through the air, it meets a range of reactions from his companions. Minelira sighs deeply in what can only be described as resignation. The elf, Vaelior, gives a knowing smirk while Beryl walks steadily, seemingly immune to the halfling's enthusiasm, perhaps plotting the quickest way to silence him.

(Verse 1)

There once was a dwarf who loved her digs,

But up she went, not down with the pigs,

She sought the sun, the skies so wide,

And found a halfling by her side!

(Chorus)

Oh, love's a funny, fickle thing,

It makes you laugh; it makes you sing!

From caves to clouds and distant parts,

It toys with our hearts.

(Verse 2)

There once was an elf who lived too long,

Who thought life was a never-ending song.

Then came a girl with years so few,

And now his heart beats anew!

(Chorus)

Oh, love's a funny thing, they say,

It finds you if you run or stay!

From endless years to fleeting days,

Love comes in many ways.

(Verse 3)

There once was a lass who loved to brawl,

She fought and won, the queen of all,

She met an elf so soft and kind,

He stole her heart and blew her mind!

(Chorus)

Oh, love's a funny, tricky thing,

It makes you laugh; it makes you sing!

From stubborn pride to gentle hands,

It knocks her where she stands!

(Verse 4)

There once was a halfling, stout and bold,

He wouldn't wed; his heart felt cold.

"No girl for me," he often jeered,

"Unless she's got a beard!"

(Chorus)

Oh, love's a funny thing, they say,

It finds you if you run or stay!

From pies and pints to hairy bliss,

You don't know what you miss!

(Final Chorus)

Oh, love's a funny, fickle thing,

It makes you wonder, makes you think!

It sneaks up always when it's due,

Love always finds you!

Beryl rolls her eyes so hard they nearly do a full circle in her skull. "Bravo!" she calls out when the song ends. "It's just like ancient poetry."

Digram beams with pride. "Really? Thank you, darling, but how?"

"Just as boring."

The human and elf laugh. Digram looks wounded, his mood darkening, a cloud that suddenly remembers it hasn't rained yet today.

"I guess no one here appreciates true artistry," he mutters, his once cheerful tone replaced by the sulky, dejected voice of someone fully convinced he is misunderstood by history. Not that history cares. His sulk softens when Minelira quickly bends to his ear and whispers, "We loved it really."

The group reaches the forest's edge, towering trees looking stern and grumpy. The air is thick with the scent of damp earth and a faint, lingering sense of mischief. Because, as we all know, any place that looks this ominous is bound to have a trick or two up its sleeve.

"Well," says Vaelior, looking up at the darkened canopy, "if there's ever a time to regret life choices, I'd say it's about now."

"Ah, nonsense," Digram says, clapping his hands together. "This is the perfect place for an adventure! Darkness, dampness, unknown dangers. It's got everything!"

"Yes," Beryl mutters, "everything except a sensible way out."

And so, with a final glance at the relatively safer world behind them, the four brave souls plunge into the forest's depths, leaving behind the warmth of the morning sun and Digram's now-fading song, which clings to the air like a stubborn echo.

3: Stone Moles

Are you afraid of the dark?

Perfect.

Now follow me into this oversized rabbit hole, though if you're expecting anything as innocent as a tea party at the end of it, temper those expectations.

You first notice the peculiar glow: four light spots floating like will-o'-the-wisps in a low, earthy tunnel. The walls and ceiling drip with the memories of countless rainy seasons. Roots dangle, resembling the skeletal fingers of some long-forgotten giant, swaying ever so slightly as if alive. Underfoot, the mud smacks and squelches in protest at being disturbed.

At the front of the group, a pale bluish light emanates from a crystal flask filled with elven magic — a photo-exothermic reaction between some overripe wisdom and the smugness of a rather snobbish race that knows, deep down, they're better than everyone else but would never say so outright. Just below it bobs a copper lantern filled with oils of unknown origin; it has a round glass window. Its golden beam cuts through the darkness like a sunray stabbing into a storm cloud.

Halfway to the ground, an ordinary red torch moves, trailing plenty of smoke, and a jar full of glowing green, dry mushrooms, so popular in the caves and mines of the lowlands, bobs alongside it. The last one is useful only for its user, just enough for eyes accustomed to the dark.

The four travellers move cautiously, their

voices reduced to whispers. There is no banter, no songs.

"Do we even know the right direction?" whispers Lady Minelira, squinting into the dim light and feeling very much disadvantaged.

"Don't worry, my love," replies Vaelior, the elf. His voice is soft and melodious, the kind of voice you trust with poetry but not necessarily with your confessions. "I'm certain the directions would not have been given to us if they were wrong."

"Well, I don't know," mutters Beryl, the dwarf. "That giant stick insect back there might have sent us into a trap. Did you see its face? It doesn't even blink. Creepy."

"Oh, come on, darling," says Digram, adjusting his pack with a grunt. "You saw Kol. He doesn't look like an untrustworthy tree to me."

"And what does an untrustworthy tree

look like?" asks Beryl, scratching her beard and glancing over her shoulder as if expecting the forest to come after them.

"My people never have much of a quarrel with trees," Digram says. "We only use fallen ones and collect dead branches for the fire. We're literally doing them a service, cremating their dead."

"I don't believe you," says Minelira.

"Are you calling me a liar?"

"No," she says, with a glint of amusement. "To lie and to not tell the truth are not the same thing."

"Shhhh . . ." Digram interrupts her and freezes mid-step, his ears twitching. The others immediately stop, instinctively listening to the silence that suddenly feels much louder than before.

"What is it, Diggie?" whispers Beryl.

"I think I hear something . . ." he

murmurs. "Though it might just be my stomach. The last time it made a noise like that was after I ate a bad turnip. Darling, what was in your pie last night?"

"Gravel," Beryl shoots back, rolling her eyes. "Don't be daft, Diggie. You nearly gave me a heart attack."

The tension eases, and they resume their careful pace, until Digram stops again, crouching by the wall.

"What's that?" he asks, pointing to a small leathery sack lying on the ground. It's covered in dirt, and no one else has noticed it.

"If it's your stomach again, I'm leaving you here," says Vaelior, not bothering to turn around.

But Digram doesn't reply. Instead, he crouches lower. "Hey, Beryl, bring your light over here. This . . . thing doesn't seem to like my fiery torch."

The others gather around, their lights illuminating the object in question: a leathery, bulbous sack about the size of a coin pouch pulsing slightly. It resembles a transparent butterfly's chrysalis, though something inside visibly struggles to break free.

"Looks like a rat," mutters Beryl, leaning closer. "Or a very angry crab trying to crawl out of a tight trap."

"Careful!" warns Vaelior, his voice tinged with alarm. "Don't touch it — it could be dangerous!"

"It's just a crab!" says Digram dismissively. "What's it going to do, pinch me to death?"

"No crab I've ever seen glows like that," Minelira muses.

The sack bursts open with a wet, squelching sound, and the creature within, something between a hairless rat and a scorpion, though with an extra pinch of nightmare for flavor, breaks free. Its twisted and sharp forelimbs stretch upwards as if grasping for an invisible sky. If you are expecting a menacing hiss or the chirp of breaks of the mine rail, you'd be disappointed. The creature turns its eyeless head towards the group, and although it makes no sound, the air around it seems to vibrate with an unsettling whine.

"Oh, that's definitely not a crab," Digram whispers, leaning back.

"No," Beryl confirms grimly. "That's worse."

No one knows why, but they all raise their heads and look up, following the yellow beam of Lady Minelira's lantern. What they see makes Digram's torch falter in his grip.

Only a metre above the head of the tallest of them, the tunnel ceiling now appears alive. The faint outlines of dozens — no, hundreds —

of leathery sacs bulge above them, each one twitching faintly. The dim light reveals wriggling forms inside, shapes moving and squirming as though testing the strength of their prisons. It seems as if a rain of disgusting newborn abominations is about to fall upon them.

"Well," says Digram, his tone somehow remaining dry even as his hand finds the hilt of his dagger. "I think we've stumbled into a nursery. And, for the record, I am not volunteering as a babysitter."

"And I say it's time to move," Minelira replies, lowering her lantern and leading the way down the corridor. Unlike other palace women, she is unafraid of mice, wasps, spiders, trolls or orcs. But she *is* scared of unfamiliar and unpredictable dangers, if not to the point of squealing, then coolly increasing the distance between them and her smooth dark skin.

"You heard the lady," Beryl growls, turning on her heel. "Let's move before these . . . things start falling."

Digram hesitates, glancing back at the lone creature. "I mean, what are the odds all of them hatch at once? Right? Maybe it's a slow-drip sort of situation."

The first sac above them ripples violently, its leathery skin splitting as a claw, disturbingly similar to the one below, slices through.

"For the love of mushrooms — run!" Digram yelps, abandoning all pretence of bravery as he bolts after Minelira.

The group breaks into a swift, uneven run, their lights bobbing wildly as they dodge roots and rocks. Behind them, faint, wet, tearing sounds fill the air, followed by the unmistakable click of claws on stone.

"Vaelior!" Minelira shouts over her shoulder, still limping slightly in her run. "Any bright ideas?"

The elf, managing to keep his composure as he runs, responds without missing a beat. "Yes! Don't look back, and hope we're faster than whatever that is!"

"Solid plan," mutters Beryl. "But I'm adding this: if something grabs me, don't come back. Just avenge me later."

"Oh, don't be dramatic, my gem," Digram huffs as he runs beside her. "I'd totally come back for you. Well, I'd think about it."

Behind them, another bag bursts, followed by a shrill crack of tearing membranes that echoes down the corridor.

"On second thought," Digram adds, his voice slightly higher now, "let's just make sure no one needs avenging!"

As the sounds of hatching and clicking grow louder, the group plunges deeper into the tunnel, the lights of their mismatched lanterns and torches flickering like stars swallowed by a gathering storm.

At last they stop, their breaths heavy and their steps reluctant, unwilling to break the eerie silence that now presses upon them. Lady Minelira raises her lantern, its light casting a cold, unwavering beam along the damp walls of the tunnel. Her eyes scan the roots and mud above them while Digram presses his wide ear to the wall. After a moment, he stands and shakes his head.

"No sounds," he declares. "If anything's following us, it's quieter than a thief in a lord's pantry."

"That's good," Beryl says, lowering her axe with a grunt. "No need to keep scurrying like frightened rabbits."

"Wait," says Lady Minelira, her tone sharp with determination. "We need to know what it is. What are we dealing with here?"

Vaelior's face darkens in thought. "A nest . . . of underground creatures," he says slowly, his words as careful as his steps had been earlier.

"Ha!" snorts Beryl. "That's what the elves used to say about our underground cities. You called them nests too."

"Only one elf, and he wasn't the wisest of our kind," Vaelior responds. "I recall tales from my youth about earth-piercing creatures. No one's seen stone moles in this century, but it seems we've stirred their offspring from some ancient slumber."

"Then the world will be hearing about them again soon," Minelira says grimly. She turns to Vaelior, placing a hand on his sleeve. "We can't just leave them there. Those . . . things will hunt the surface dwellers of all sorts. We must go back and deal with them."

"Oh no!" Digram interjects with a note of unease. "They're just babies. They're no bigger than puppies."

"Did you see how many there were?" Minelira's gaze is fierce. "They'll grow, and they'll kill. People, livestock, dwarves ... everything."

"Especially dwarves," Beryl mutters. "Elves might tiptoe lightly enough to avoid notice, but we stomp. Let's go back and end this before it starts."

It is not a pleasant decision, but they all know it is necessary. Steeling themselves, they retrace their steps towards the nest.

When they arrive, they are greeted by a far more dreadful sight. The sacs have burst entirely, and the creatures within, although considerably fewer, have already doubled in size, their twisted forms crawling through the blood-red mud. They lunge at one another, claws flashing, tearing into flesh. The victors devour the defeated, their grotesque forms swelling even larger with every bite.

"Curious," Vaelior murmurs, his silver eyes narrowing. "A brutal kind of natural selection. Soon, only one will remain — the largest, strongest and far more dangerous. It will dig new tunnels and hunt the surface."

"It's terrible," Digram mutters, his face pale. "And I almost feel sorry for them."

"Darling, do something," Minelira urges. "They're growing so quickly."

Vaelior nods, stepping forwards. "Stand back," he says, his voice calm but commanding. "Digram, my friend, might I borrow your flame?"

With some reluctance, the halfling hands over his torch. Vaelior grips it firmly in his left hand while raising his right hand above his head, and his fingers splay wide.

Reader, I cannot repeat what he intones; his voice is melodic yet forceful, as he speaks in a language as old as the world itself. It is one I have never learned.

The red torchlight wavers, then turns a brilliant blue, its brightness casting eerie shadows that dance across the tunnel walls. With a swift motion, Vaelior sweeps his hand towards the creatures. The blue flame leaps from the torch, swelling into a wave of fire that engulfs the writhing horrors. There is no screeching, no screams of agony. Only the crackling of burning flesh and the sharp, dry pops of their brittle limbs collapsing into ash. When the flames subside, only a blackened pile of twisted remains is left, the air thick with smoke so foul it seems to poison their very souls.

"Can we get out of here now?" Beryl mutters, covering her mouth. "Diggie, darling, if you're not planning on reading a funeral oration over them . . ."

But Digram takes back his torch without a

word. He turns and starts down the tunnel, his light bouncing along the walls. The others exchange glances before following him, the silence heavier than ever.

"Well," Minelira finally says softly, "that was . . . decisive."

Beryl falls in step beside her. "Efficient too. I mean, say what you like about elves, but they don't mess around with their magic."

"True," Minelira replies, glancing back at Vaelior walking at a measured pace behind them. "Though I never see him being so easy about setting things on fire."

"Don't worry about him," Beryl says with a smirk. "Elves love a good dramatic flourish."

At the rear of the group, Vaelior arches an elegant eyebrow but says nothing, letting the murmur of their conversation drift ahead. Digram finally breaks his silence as they continue down the tunnel.

"You know," he begins, his voice low. "Little things don't ask to be born."

Minelira touches his shoulder lightly as she passes. "Let's not forget what they'd grow into. Sometimes kindness is doing the hard thing before it gets worse."

Digram sighs but nods. "You're right, my lady. But let it be known: I officially do not like this adventure any more. I vote for a treasure chest or a friendly inn next."

"Noted," Vaelior replies drily, catching up with the group. "Though I must say, Digram Oldbook, your dislike of this adventure has coincided nicely with your fear of the dark."

"That's called prudence," Digram counters. "And also, what I like to call survival instincts. Something we short folk are very good at, by the way."

"Let's hope those instincts lead us somewhere with fresher air," Beryl mutters.

"Because if that smoke gets into our clothes, even the orcs will think we smell bad."

The group's banter resumes as they press on. Behind them, the blackened remains of the stone moles lie in silence, a grim reminder of what was nearly unleashed.

4: Silly Con

Reader, do you smell that? Disgusting, isn't it? It remind me of forgotten damp laundry that has a hard time drying on its own.

The elf, whose sensitive nose detects the odour first, winces slightly but says nothing in typical elven fashion. He merely presses forwards. Then the halfling sneezes — a sudden, explosive sound that echoes through the cavern, followed by an irritated grunt.

"Ugh," mutters Beryl, her voice muffled as she buries her face in her beard. "This too much, even for me."

Lady Minelira asks, "What time of day do you think it is up there, on the surface?"

"I'd wager late afternoon," replies

Digram. "And by the sound of it, we've missed lunch. Likely dinner, too, at this rate."

"I've lost my appetite," Lord Vaelior responds coldly.

The halfling, however, is less composed. "I might have as well, but long fasting can lead to dire consequences for one's health."

"You're concerned about everyone's health, I hope?" Beryl asks. "Not just your own?"

"Of course, my dear," Digram replies, his tone honeyed. "I'm thinking of all of us, particularly my beloved—"

"Hold on a moment," interrupts Minelira, her voice cutting through the bickering like a blade. "Doesn't the tunnel feel . . . wider?"

The company halts, their heads lifting as one. The dim lantern light reveals that, indeed, the tunnel has grown more spacious. The ceiling, once so low it could almost graze Vaelior's head, now looms high above, and its surface is lost in shadow. The walls, which had hemmed them in with oppressive closeness, now widen with each step until the space resembles a vast underground hall.

"Looks like we've stumbled into something bigger," Beryl grumbles, her fingers tightening on her axe.

"Wonderful," Digram mutters, clutching his torch as though it might shield him from whatever lies ahead. "Perhaps it's a banquet hall for the creatures we just roasted."

Beryl steps forwards. "Be wary," she says. "Such spaces are rarely empty, and the builders of these halls are not often hospitable."

Minelira tilts her lantern, casting its light further into the expanse. Shadows leap and dance, revealing jagged rock formations just like broken bones. The faint glimmer of moisture on the walls hints at underground streams or something less innocent.

"Do you think this is where they lived?" asks Minelira, her voice barely above a whisper.

"No, my love," Vaelior replies. "This is not a lair. It feels . . . older. Ancient, even."

Beryl gives a curt nod. "Aye. The stones here have stories. I don't like the sound of them."

Digram, ever eager to lighten the mood, clears his throat. "Well, if it's ancient, perhaps there's treasure. A bit of gold would make this journey more tolerable, wouldn't it?"

But even his jest falls flat. They move forwards cautiously, their steps echoing in the vast emptiness, every sound a reminder of how small they are in this strange and silent world.

The cavern looms vast and echoing, a space so ancient it seems to hold the memory of the earth's first hiccup. Some glowing animals, resembling snails, cover the rocks. Stalactites hang from the unseen ceiling like the fangs of some great beast, and the small pools scattered across the floor gleam with an oily, malevolent sheen in the pale light of their torches. The air is thick and oppressive. Somewhere in the darkness, a damp, rhythmic breath rises and falls; each exhale sending ripples through the pools. It is not just a sound but a presence, a heavy awareness that crawls over the neck and whispers, "You do not belong here."

"Hm," murmurs Digram, breaking the uneasy silence. His gaze is fixed on the largest of the pools, the water surface trembling as if in anticipation. "Well, that's ominous."

Beryl snorts softly. "What gave it away, Diggie?"

Vaelior silences them with a raised hand, his keen elven eyes scanning the shadows at the far side of the cavern. "Quiet," he says softly. "Something stirs."

The group tenses, their lights swinging towards where the elf's gaze is fixed. At first, the darkness seems impenetrable, but then a shape emerges, shifting sluggishly through the gloom. Its movements are vast, hunched, ponderous, yet purposeful. It wades through the largest pool, the liquid lapping at its midsection and sending oily waves rippling outwards. A faint, wet glint on its hide suggests fur matted with some unwholesome sludge.

"What in the ten's kingdom is that?" whispers Minelira, her lantern shaking slightly in her grasp.

"A troll. But not a very big one," Vaelior observes, his voice calm but edged with wariness.

"A baby troll?" Minelira asks.

"There is no such thing," the elf replies. "Trolls are born fully formed from the rocky earth, as ancient as the stone that births them. They do not grow. That one," he adds, nodding towards the hulking figure, "looks old and desperate. Starving, perhaps, if it's reduced to digging through those pools for worms and slugs."

"And we're the perfect addition to its diet," mutters Beryl, eyeing the troll with grim determination. "Old or not, it's still a troll. And it's still got claws the size of my axe blade."

"Let's not jump to conclusions," says Digram, though his voice carries more optimism than certainty. He adjusts his belt and attempts a casual shrug, though the sweat beading on his brow gives him away. "Maybe he's just here for a nice swim. You know, a bit of self-care in the mud bath."

Beryl shoots him a look. "A troll? Self-care? What next, a dragon looking for a pedicure?"

"Well," Digram counters, "if one —"

"Quiet," Vaelior interrupts sharply.

The troll has stopped rummaging in the

pools and now stands motionless, its massive, sodden head tilted towards them. Even without eyes as sharp as the elf's, the group can feel its attention.

The troll climbs out of the pool and sniffs the air, a wet, guttural sound reverberating through the cavern. Its claws, black and jagged as broken obsidian, flex against the stone floor, leaving shallow gouges in their wake. Slowly, it turns, revealing a mouth bristling with teeth that look better suited for crushing rock than chewing flesh.

"I suppose he's done swimming for now," Digram murmurs.

Minelira's voice is low and sharp. "Vaelior, what do we do?"

"We stay calm," the elf replies, his tone unyielding. "Trolls are territorial, not mindless. If we don't provoke it—"

The creature lets out a deep, guttural

noise, something between a growl and a boulder grinding against stone. It takes the first step towards the group, sending tremors through the ground.

"Well," says Digram, taking a cautious step back, "I think it's fair to say we've been noticed."

Beryl assumes a battle position. "Noticed? It's sizing us up for the menu, Diggie."

"Or it's curious," Minelira says, drawing her sword.

"Curiosity gets trolls killed," Beryl growls, raising her axe.

Vaelior's hand goes to his bow, his gaze never leaving the advancing troll. "Hold your ground. Trolls may be strong, but they are slow. If it charges, aim for its legs. A troll cannot fight on its knees."

"Comforting," Minelira mutters. "But what happens if there's more than one?"

The elf's jaw tightens.

The troll takes another step forwards, its movements deliberate and unhurried. Then it pauses, sniffing the air, and lets out another deep, rumbling growl.

"Right," Vaelior says quietly. "Everyone, be ready. But don't strike unless it charges."

"Define *charges*," Digram mutters, shifting his torch to his left hand while fumbling for the dagger at his belt.

The troll crouches slightly as if preparing to spring, its muscles coiling beneath its wet, glistening hide.

"That's charging," Beryl says, her axe swinging up.

"Agreed," Minelira says, raising her sword.

The troll roars — a sound so deep it feels like the cavern itself has burped — and begins to run. But three ponderous steps in, it skids and stops right in front of the travellers, one bony leg still lifted.

"Now ... hang on!" bellows the troll, flailing one enormous hand. His voice was unexpectedly high, trembling and unpleasant, like the voice of a market trader. "I'm not here to eat you!"

The silence that follows is palpable. The group exchanges glances, their weapons raised.

"Not ... here to eat us?" Digram repeats, his voice tinged with disbelief.

The troll puts his foot down and sighs a long, exaggerated sigh. "Honestly, why does everyone always assume? It's very prejudiced, you know. Terribly bad for interspecies relations."

"That's ... unusual," Lady Minelira says, her voice low.

The troll huffs, its bony chest puffing out indignantly. "Well, I can't eat you, can I?

Healer's orders. Low calcium diet. Something about bone density problems. She says no more crunchy things, and your lot looks far too crunchy."

Beryl lowers her weapon an inch. "Crunchy?" she repeats, her tone as sharp as her blade.

"Yes, crunchy!" the troll snaps. "Look at you! Armour, weapons, that thick beard of yours. You'd be murder on my molars. And don't even suggest the halfling. Too many pies, I'd wager. All pastry and no protein. It's like chewing on a stale biscuit."

"Excuse me!" Digram sputters, clutching at his middle. "This is prime halfling muscle, thank you very much."

The troll ignores him and continues. "The healer says I must cut back on stringy meat, too. So that's you, Mr Tall Elf," he says, pointing a long, bony finger at Vaelior. "Can't eat lean either, which rules out you, Lady Fancy Lantern."

"Lean?" Minelira mutters, her grip still firm on her sword.

The troll cocks his huge head conspiratorially. "I'm mostly on a liquid diet these days. Sludge smoothies, worm broth, maybe the occasional slug terrine if I'm feeling fancy."

The group stares at him, dumbfounded.

"Well, this is a new one," Beryl says. "We're not in danger of being eaten because you've got . . . dietary restrictions?"

"It's not a restriction," the troll says, clearly offended. "It's a lifestyle choice. Troll health is no joke, you know. All that rubbish can clog the system. Gotta keep things moving."

"I can't believe we're being judged by a troll on our edibility," mutters Digram.

"Don't take it personally," the troll says

with a shrug that dislodges a small stalactite from the ceiling. "It's not about you; it's about me. My gut's a delicate ecosystem."

"Can we . . . go now?" Vaelior asks.

"Of course, of course," the troll says magnanimously. "But I came to you with a warning. If you're heading that way," he points one gnarled claw towards the well-lit end of the cavern, where the pools shimmer like liquid night, "stay to the left. The right side is a breeding ground for many-leggers. You're too crunchy for me, sure, but to them, you're a walking cocktail. And if you see anything with more limbs than you can count, keep still. Don't run."

Vaelior finally takes the arrow off his bow, though his expression remains sceptical. "Why help us?"

The troll gives a rumbling chuckle. "Why not? I'm not in the mood for company, alive or otherwise. Good thing you're carrying light. Nasty things don't like light. Stick together, and you might just leave here in one piece."

The group hesitates a moment longer before Digram coughs politely. "Uh . . . thanks?"

"Don't mention it," the troll says, turning to go. "Now, if you'll excuse me, I need a nap. Too much excitement for one day."

"What is your name?" Minelira asks.

"They call me Silly Con. Don't tell anyone you met a helpful troll. I've got a reputation to maintain."

And with that, the troll walks away into the darkness, leaving the adventurers to exchange bewildered looks in the flickering light of their torches. Before the broad back disappears into the darkness, Vaelior raises his bow, pulls the bowstring, and . . . doesn't shoot, slowly lowering it instead and returning it behind his back.

Digram exhales noisily.

"Well," Beryl says at last, "I've been insulted by humans, mocked by elves, fellow dwarves and shot at by orcs, but being turned down as a meal by a health-conscious troll? That's a new one."

"Look on the bright side, my gem," Digram says, adjusting his pack. "At least we're not dinner."

"Not dinner," Minelira says with a wry smile. "We are just . . . crunchy."

"I could have killed him," Vaelior says thoughtfully. "Why didn't I?"

"Well . . . he is kind of . . . adorable," Digram says.

"Diggie, you have bizarre taste. We all know that." Minelira smiles. "By the way, did anyone notice that this cave smells awful? Like a wet cloth or something?"

5: Run

The oppressive gloom of the cave gradually gives way to an almost ethereal glow.

Bioluminescent snails cling to every surface — walls, ceilings and even the jagged edges of forgotten columns. Their shimmering light transforms the dungeon into a hall that could be mistaken for a misplaced ballroom, were it not for the damp chill.

You notice this, too, my dear readers, don't you? I do wonder what our heroes make of this peculiar development.

It's Beryl who breaks the silence first, her voice carrying the familiar gruff authority of someone who has no patience for nonsense. "What's this now? Diggie, put out that torch. We must conserve fuel, not waste it competing with these slimy lanterns. You, too, you beanpoles," she adds, gesturing at the tall Vaelior and Minelira. "We're sorely lacking practicality here."

They snuff out their lights one by one until the only illumination comes from the vibrant snail colonies casting their ghostly glow. Lady Minelira suddenly pauses, her hand resting lightly on the wall.

"We need to stop and rest," she says. "Why don't we sit for an hour and rest our legs? My blisters are killing me."

Vaelior turns to her, concern flickering across his face. "What's wrong, my love?"

"Nothing," she replies, though her expression betrays a hint of relief. "I think we've finally left that dreadful stench far enough behind."

"Aye," Beryl mutters, her nose wrinkling

at the memory. "It was like a troll's shorts after a thunderstorm."

"Or an orc's idea of perfume," adds Digram, crouching down and pointing at something on the ground. "And look here, these marks. I've noticed them since it started getting lighter."

Vaelior kneels beside him, his sharp elven eyes tracing the faint grooves. "You are correct, my well-observant friend. Something passed through here, dragging ... or being dragged. Thoughts?"

"Not yet," Digram admits, his brow furrowing. "Do you think it's recent?"

Vaelior doesn't answer immediately. He tilts his head, listening to the cavern's faint echoes, then runs his fingers through the muck. "Recent enough," he says finally. He gestures to the countless tiny holes lining either side of the scrape marks. "And look here. What do these remind you of?"

Digram squints. "Tracks of centipedes?"

"Precisely," Vaelior says, his tone grave. "They drag their long bodies. Small legs, no matter how many, cannot lift that weight from the ground."

"Many-leggers?" Minelira's voice rises slightly, betraying her unease. "But that troll said they lived in another cavern and that we'd be safe if we stayed to the left!"

"Well," Vaelior says drily, "it seems the troll lied. Here they are, heading that way." He gestures towards the faint outline of an archway in the distance.

"Wonderful," Digram mutters. "We're walking straight into their living room. I'll let you do the introductions, my lord."

Beryl gives him a sharp nudge, her expression grim. "Quiet, Diggie. No time for jokes when there's axe work coming."

Minelira tightens her grip on her sword. "We're not actually going that way, are we? I don't mind slicing orcs, but those ... those creepy things are—"

"—as fat as my grandmother, and gods know how long," Beryl finishes. "We don't know how they fight, but I'm not keen to be their cocktail or whatever else they might be after."

Vaelior stands, brushing his hands off on his cloak. "That troll tricked us," he says. "He's no Silly Con; he's a con artist."

"We were fools to believe his silly tale about his diet," Digram says with a frown. "I should've known."

Minelira's eyes flash. "Let's go back and kill him. I can't imagine standing there and scolding him with 'shame on you.'"

Beryl checks her blade for sharpness with her thumb. "I'm with her. Let's cut out the middleman before we're the main course."

Vaelior sighs. "Killing him might solve one problem, but it doesn't change what lies ahead."

"Well," Digram says, glancing warily at the archway, "it's either back to the troll or forwards to the centipedes. Pick your poison."

"Forwards," Vaelior decides firmly, his tone brooking no argument. "If we go back, we'll waste time and the troll will be expecting us. It's better to face whatever lies ahead while we still have the element of surprise."

"Surprise, is it?" Digram mutters. "That's one word for it. I can think of a few others far less optimistic. Gem of my eyes," he adds, turning to Beryl, "what do your people say about those many-leggers? Fire, perhaps? Or a rousing dwarven ballad? Surely there's some trick to dealing with them."

Beryl shrugs, the nonchalance doing little to mask her unease. "Not much to tell. We didn't see them often in the deep mines, but I've heard tales. They're big, fast as a man."

Minelira, perched elegantly on a low rock, looks up, her dark eyes sparkling with intrigue. "As fast? Or faster?" she asks.

"Not sure," Beryl admits. "At least faster than a dwarf. We're built for endurance, not speed. Not all of us have your long legs, princess."

"Hmmm . . ." Minelira's gaze drifts to her husband. Vaelior catches the look and raises a brow.

"You're scheming again, my love," he says, the faintest trace of amusement tugging at his lips. "Let me guess. 'Help Us, Old Wizard'?"

"Something like that," Minelira replies, a sly smile forming.

Beryl furrows her brow. "What in the stone's name is 'Help Us, Old Wizard'?"

"Oh, I know this one!" Digram grins, his

wiry features alight. "It's from their early orc-hunting days. A trick to lure something nasty into a trap. Usually involves someone fast enough to outrun the beast."

"But this isn't orcs," Beryl points out flatly. "And where's the trap?"

Minelira's smile deepens. "The troll."

"You're joking, my lady!" Digram blurts.

"I am not," Minelira says coolly. "Vaelior and I will lead the centipedes to the troll. They deserve each other. You two stay somewhere safe and keep watch."

With some effort — and no shortage of muttered complaints — Digram and Beryl clamber onto a high ledge. There, they settle themselves as quietly as possible, their weapons ready. Below, the eerie luminescence of glowing snails dances across the cavern walls, casting shifting, spectral shapes.

They see Vaelior and Minelira move

stealthily towards the far archway, their steps near-silent on the damp stone. The cavern swallows them up, its glow fading as they disappear from sight.

Minutes pass. Digram gets bored and starts to murmur a new song quietly, melodic and slow like a lullaby:

Through the tunnels and shadows deep,
Where stone-bound secrets lie asleep,
A halfling sings to light the way,
I hope we'll see another day!
Oh, caves so cold, and dark, and grim,
We'll face your depths; we won't give in!
Though snails may glow, and trolls may stare,
Our torches blaze; we'll take the dare!

"Keep it down," Beryl mutters. "Sing loud enough, and you'll have every cave beast from here to the mountain's root joining in."

"Now that would make for an

entertaining chorus," Digram replies with a cheeky grin, but he stops singing.

More time passes.

Beryl sniffs. "This was a bad idea, Diggie."

"Why, my gem?" Digram asks, his eyes shut as if he had dozed off already.

"Because we'll never see them again," she says grimly. "And unless you plan to jump down from here without shattering both legs, we're doomed, too."

Digram opens his eyes and mouth to reply but freezes. His ears prick up. "Wait. Do you hear that?"

"Hear what?"

At first, it's no more than a faint hum, a vibration that thrums through the rock. Then it grows — a low, resonant rumble that crawls up their spines, setting their bones on edge.

Suddenly, Vaelior reappears, gliding with

the effortless grace of his kind, Minelira hot on his heels, her limp forgotten. They dash past the ledge like a gust of wind, Minelira calling over her shoulder, "Mind the herd traffic, dears!"

And then the tide comes.

A wave of creatures bursts into view, surging like a river of nightmares. Each centipede, reddish-brown with glistening black segments, is longer than a fishing boat, its countless legs churning in a grotesque rhythm. The cavern fills with their movement, the chittering and scraping blending into a deafening roar.

Beryl's beard sweeps up, her braids like whips. Her curls billow wildly, and even she, steadfast and stone-hearted as any dwarf, clutches the ledge and her husband with trembling hands. Beside her, Digram flattens himself against the rock face.

The cacophony defies description in *this*

world. Yet, if you or I were there, we might liken it to the roar of a night express. A locomotive of chaos and dread stripped of the comforting whistle and steady glow of its lights.

Dozens upon dozens of creatures pour past, their singular focus on the fleeing figures of Vaelior and Minelira. The vibrations rattle the stone, the air and their very bones.

"Dinner and a show," Digram shouts, squinting, though his voice barely carries above the din. "Darling, you are breaking my arm!"

"Quiet." Beryl hisses, her knuckles white around his wrist. "Just . . . quiet."

6: Hunger Against Hunger

Vaelior's sharp eyes adjust quickly to the gloom as he and Minelira enter, still running shoulder to shoulder into the shadowed expanse of the troll's lair. The air here is heavy and damp with the stench of stagnant water and something more primal. Black, glistening pools dot the uneven cavern floor, their surfaces reflecting distorted fragments of pale light from the passage behind them.

There, in the dark, Silly Con the troll prowls. His massive frame is hunched, his shaggy, mud-slick body blending with the stone. He moves with a lumbering purpose, pausing to sniff the air or rake a clawed hand through one of the pools in search of anything eatable.

Anything. Hunger drives his every motion. But then the noise of the oncoming many-leggers echoes through the cavern. Vaelior notices the troll freeze, his hulking form rigid with horror.

Minelira's breathing is laboured from running. "Do we have a further plan?" she asks. "We lure the many-leggers here. Then what?"

Vaelior hesitates. "I confess, I didn't think this far ahead."

Minelira gives him a sidelong glance, a wry smile curving her lips despite the pain. "I love you for your honesty, my lord."

"I prefer not to lie when we're running towards a huge troll," Vaelior replies, his breathing steady as though they have been walking, not sprinting. His gaze darts upwards, taking in the cavern's jagged ceiling. Stalactites hang low from above, and nearby, a cluster of stone columns rises from the floor, their tops disappearing into the blackness above. An idea sparks.

Without a word, Vaelior nocks an arrow to his bowstring, his stride never faltering. Minelira catches on immediately, moving closer as he aims.

"Be ready," he says.

The arrow flies true, embedding itself into the side of a thick column with a satisfying thump, three or four metres above the ground. Without slowing, Vaelior wraps an arm firmly around Minelira's waist.

"Now."

She pushes off the ground in a jump, wrapping her arms and legs around his body. Vaelior does something no human could. He runs up the vertical column's side like level ground. In a heartbeat, he grabs the arrow protruding from the rock with one hand, still holding his wife securely with the other.

They hang there, motionless, as a living

flood of furious creatures pours into the cavern below. Silly Con turns towards the noise, his beady eyes narrowing, claws flexing in readiness.

The first wave hits, and the battle begins.

The troll roars, a sound that shakes the cavern walls, and lashes out with a massive arm. His claws catch one of the centipede's mid-lunge, tearing it apart in a spray of black ichor. Another creature darts towards his legs, and the troll kicks out, sending it into a pool with a wet splash.

But for every centipede he crushes, two more surge forwards. Silly Con fights ferociously, his strength unmatched, but the tide is relentless. The many-leggers swarm over him, their mandibles clacking, their bodies writhing and curling around his limbs.

Vaelior watches in silence, his expression unreadable. Minelira clings to him, her face pale but resolute.

"They'll kill this troll," she murmurs. "But not before Silly Con takes most of them with him."

Vaelior nods, his eyes following the brutal exchange below. The troll's growls become hoarse, and its movements slow. Still, he fights on, crushing and flinging centipedes with a pitiful tenacity.

Finally, with one last ear-splitting scream, the troll collapses, his massive body half sinking into the largest pool. The centipedes swarm over it, their chittering echoing in the cavern as they feast on its fluids.

Then the creatures begin to retreat as quickly as they have come. One by one, they skitter away, vanishing into the darkness. The cavern falls silent, save for the soft hiss of bubbles in the pools.

Vaelior exhales slowly, his grip relaxing.

Minelira glances up at him. "Do you think they're gone for good?"

"For now," he says quietly. "But I wouldn't trust them not to return."

"Are we jumping down?" Minelira asks.

"Not yet." Vaelior looks into her brown eyes, a smile tugging at his lips. "We've never kissed hanging from an arrow."

"Yes, we have. Remember the broken bridge and the waterfall, the Mother's Tears?"

"Oh yes, but that wasn't above dead enemies."

"True . . ." With that, Minelira reaches up and kisses him long and passionately.

Vaelior, reluctant to let go of the arrow, feels it suddenly snap beneath their weight. They tumble to the ground in a tangle of limbs. Vaelior lands first, twisting mid-fall to turn on his back and catch Minelira against his chest.

They kiss again, laughter bubbling

between them despite the chaos of the cavern. After a moment, they disentangle and get to their feet, their expressions turning serious as they return to the task at hand.

The troll lies motionless. His lifeless bulk is half submerged in an oily pool. He is still alive when the couple approaches. Shrunken and hollow, the troll's body looks as if every drop of fluid has been drained from it. He opens his desiccated eyes, sensing them.

"They would have left your ... lovely, crunchy corpses for me ... tasty ... crunchy ..." he rasps before trailing into silence. Within moments, his remains crumble into a dry, shapeless pile of clay.

Vaelior spares the heap one last glance before turning away. "Come, my love," he says. "Our work here is done. Let's collect the others and leave this place before many-leggers get hungry again and return."

Minelira's limp is worse than before. The inside of her boot is wet with blood, and if the damn woman doesn't tell her husband about it, I will.

7: Axes and Daggers

Minelira adjusts her grip on Vaelior's hand as they retrace their steps to the brighter, more spacious cave. The luminescent snails bathe the walls and ceiling in an otherworldly glow, and for a moment, the sight feels almost serene. But as they approach the ledge where their companions have hidden, her eyes catch movement.

"Look," she whispers, releasing Vaelior's hand and pointing upwards.

It looks like one of the many-leggers has lingered behind. Its sinuous body coils and uncoils as it scales the rock face. It's smaller, no longer than a cart, but still deadly. It's halfway up the climb, its wriggling legs finding purchase with disturbing ease.

Above it, Beryl and Digram stand on their precarious perch. The dwarf is poised, her broad-shouldered frame tense, gripping her weapon with both hands. Digram, in contrast, seems less sure of himself.

Minelira folds her arms and leans lightly against Vaelior. "Shall we help?" she asks, her voice low and teasing.

"Nah," Vaelior replies, his gaze fixed on the unfolding scene. "I am sure that thing can manage that rock just fine."

Minelira giggles and checks her sword. Both the halfling and the dwarf are clever in their ways. "Five coppers say Beryl handles it alone," she murmurs.

"I don't gamble, my love," Vaelior says evenly, though his lips twitch in what might be a suppressed smile.

The many-legger surges higher, its body

rippling like dark silk, and Beryl finally moves. With a guttural yell, she swings her axe downwards. The weapon gleams briefly in the cave's light before embedding in one of the creature's legs. A shrill, unnatural screech echoes through the cavern, making Minelira wince.

The many-legger writhes, but its grip holds firm. It lashes upwards, one of its front mandibles striking perilously close to Digram's boot. The halfling yelps, hopping back and nearly losing his balance.

"Oh, come now, Diggie," Minelira murmurs under her breath, amused.

Beryl doesn't falter. She yanks her axe free and strikes again, this time severing another of the creature's legs. Black ichor sprays the rock, but the many-legger doesn't retreat. If anything, its writhing becomes more frantic as it scrambles closer.

"Throw something, Digram Oldbook!"

Beryl barks, her voice carrying clearly to Minelira and Vaelior.

Digram blinks, his gaze darting around. Then he fumbles at his belt and produces his dagger. He hesitates just long enough for Beryl to snap, "Now!"

The halfling flings the knife with surprising precision. It strikes the creature squarely between its clustered eyes, entering flesh with an unpleasant wet sound. The many-legger convulses violently, its legs splaying outwards before it releases its grip on the rock and plummets to the cavern floor with a resounding thud.

Beryl lets out a satisfied huff, planting her axe on her shoulder. "Well, that's sorted," she says, glancing at Digram, who looks both relieved and slightly nauseous.

From their vantage point below, Vaelior gives Minelira a sidelong glance. "I'll collect my coppers now."

"I thought you don't gamble."

He shrugs and nods at their companions. "We should join them. They'll be wanting to leave this place quickly, I think."

Minelira gives a sigh of mock disappointment. "And here I thought we'd enjoy the spectacle a little longer."

"Plenty of time for that later," Vaelior says, offering her his hand. "Are you sure I shouldn't carry you?"

"Thank you, I can manage," Minelira replies, wincing slightly but leaning on his arm with gratitude.

Together, they cross the cavern floor towards their weary but victorious friends, the faintly glowing snails casting shifting patterns over the fight's aftermath.

As soon as the heroes regroup, rest, share some flat bread from Vaelior's backpack, and exchange their accounts of the event, they continue their journey towards the goal we are still to learn about.

Phew! I don't know about you, but I feel a little overwhelmed with worries about them. Although, who, if not I, knew that they would be just fine?

8: The Healer of Noon-Fogs

It takes a while to adjust to the darkness again, doesn't it? Thankfully, the four colourful dots of light — blue, yellow, green and red — bloom anew, illuminating the winding cave path. Each glow casts its own peculiar hue, turning the walls into a shifting mosaic of earthen tones. And do I hear that right? Of course, our halfling is singing again, the flickering flame of his red torch blackening the stone walls with soot. His voice, soft and low, drifts through the air, just barely audible. He knows better than to belt out his tune here. Beryl would box his ears if he dared disturb the uneasy silence of these depths.

Yet, there's something almost comforting

in the rhythm of his song, a quiet rebellion against the weight of the oppressive dark. While largely nonsense, the words carry a warm, lilting melody that threads through the group's uneasy hearts.

You can be brave, you can be strong,

But wits will often right the wrong.

Why face a dragon you can't outfight,

When a clever trick could save the night?

I'll outpace the storm on a horse's stride,

Set fleas on wolves till they run and hide.

I'll rouse the bees to harry the bear,

And steal the honey from its lair.

But my heart's desire, my truest call,

Is not in tricks or wits at all.

For my sweet girl, with her gaze so bright,

Would love me best if I stand and fight.

So steel in hand and eye kept keen,

I'll face the beast where none have been.

Though quick wits aid, and tricks are sly,

For her, I'd fight or even die.

Beryl softly hushes him occasionally, though a faint, loving smile tugs at her lips.

Once again, Vaelior walks silently at the front, illuminated by the blue light of his elvish crystal. Behind him, Lady Minelira holds her lantern high, its golden beam steady and resolute. She occasionally glances back, her expression unreadable.

The deeper they go, the colder the air becomes. It clings to their skin as if the rocks themselves are pressing down on them.

"Feels like we are descending into the belly of the world," Beryl mutters, her voice rough but steady. "And yet, I can tell we're going up, not down."

"That's because it's true," Vaelior replies

without turning. "I think we've reached the end of the underground part of our journey, my friends. Look." He points ahead, his keen eyes fixed on a different kind of darkness between the rocky folds. This isn't the suffocating black of the cave's depths but an inky expanse pricked with tiny, distant lights.

"Are those stars?" Minelira's voice rings faintly in the silence of the cave.

"No wonder I'm exhausted. It's past midnight!" Digram exclaims with relief.

"I wouldn't rush out just yet. Let's make sure it's safe outside," Beryl says, her tone as practical as ever. She turns to her husband. "Diggie."

"Yes, dear?" Digram replies a bit too innocently.

"What are you waiting for?"

"Oh . . . yes. I'm going, I'm going," the halfling mutters, extinguishing his torch. He shuffles forwards on his bare feet, moving with the halfling's innate stealth. He approaches the cave exit and parts the thick shrubs blocking their view.

"Apart from a bramble that's seen better days, I see no danger," he announces, stepping through.

The others begin to follow, but before Beryl can take more than a step, they freeze at the sound of a short, sharp scream.

Beryl surges forwards without hesitation and is the next to emerge. Moments later the rest of the group stands together on the slope of a hill bathed in silver moonlight. Sparse trees dot the landscape, their almost leafless, skeletal forms swaying in the wind.

The torch lies smoking at their feet, its charred tip still warm. But Digram is nowhere to be seen.

"Digram?" Beryl's voice is sharp, carrying

a weight that only years of worry and affection can lend. She steps forwards. "If this is one of your pranks, I swear I will— Diggie?" she calls again, her voice softening but no less urgent.

Minelira steps closer, raising her lantern. The steady beam of light cuts through the thickets but finds no trace of the halfling. "He was just here," she says, her voice faltering slightly. "He stepped out first. There wasn't time for—"

"The scream," Vaelior interrupts. He crouches near the torch, his long fingers brushing the disturbed ground. "Something moved quickly. There's a trail in the tall grass. Something took him."

"Something took him?" Beryl echoes, her voice hardening with fury. "What could take a halfling so quickly and leave nothing but a smoking torch? Orcs are not known for their agility."

"A predator," Vaelior replies grimly. "And one that knows this terrain well."

"Or worse," Minelira mutters, glancing at the thick darkness beyond the trees. "Something clever."

Beryl's voice shakes as she eyes the woods around them. "We're going after him."

"Of course we are," Vaelior says. "But not without some strategy. If we rush in without a plan, we might join him wherever he's been taken."

"I don't need a plan," Beryl growls. "I need my husband."

"And we need all of us alive to get him back," Vaelior counters, his calm tone carrying an edge of authority.

Before Beryl can retort, Minelira steps between them. "We'll follow the tracks," she says firmly. "Beryl, your axe will do no good if you charge headlong into an ambush. Let's move together, carefully. For Digram's sake."

Beryl hesitates, her jaw clenched, but finally nods. "Fine. But if anything so much as breathes wrong, it's getting this iron in its skull."

"That's the spirit," Minelira says with an encouraging smile. She glances at Vaelior. "*You*'re our tracker now, my lord."

Vaelior does not hesitate. "This way," he says, moving quickly but quietly along a furrow in the grass, the others close behind.

As they descend into the shadowy grove, the night grows heavier, the stars above obscured by the thick canopy. The silence is broken only by the occasional rustle of leaves and the faint crunch of their boots on the forest floor. The trail grows fainter, but Vaelior presses on, his elvish eyes searching for signs unseen by the others.

Then a low, guttural growl comes from the darkness ahead. A sound that stops them all in their tracks.

The forest is alive with the flicker of a distant, vast campfire. Its light dances through the thick trees. The crackle of flames carries on the wind, mingling with a high-pitched, screechy voice that grates on the ears. Beneath it all is an unsettling sound, like a dog squealing in protest.

Beryl strains against Vaelior's grip. "He must be there," she hisses. "I know it. Let me go!"

"Wait," Vaelior whispers sharply, his tone brooking no argument. "Rushing in will do him no good. Patience, Beryl."

Minelira crouches beside her, placing a steadying hand on her shoulder. "Listen," she urges softly. "We'll get him, but we need to know what we're up against first."

Reluctantly, Beryl obeys, her breath heavy with suppressed fury. The group creeps forwards, careful not to snap twigs or brush too loudly against the undergrowth. As they draw nearer, the voice becomes clearer.

"How many times do I have to tell you — I don't want orcs," the voice whines, shrill and indignant. "They're just not the right ingredient and too bony. I need fat for this remedy to work."

A sharp, squealing yelp cuts through the air, followed by an impatient sigh.

"Okay, this one is not so bony," the voice admits grudgingly.

Another squeal comes, this time with a low, rumbling growl beneath it.

"And not so much orc, either. What on Mid-Earth have you brought me, Fluffy?"

A snarl answers, followed by more growls.

"What now? Orcs in the woods? Nice try. I say . . . I say I might be able to use this thing somehow, but not this time."

The growl deepens into a threatening rumble.

"Oh, pucker it in, Fluffy!" the voice snaps, followed by a sharp thwack. "Go that way this time and bring me a wild pig like last time. Go on, off with you!"

There is the thump of something massive galloping away, its footfalls shaking the ground faintly.

Then, after a moment of eerie calm, the voice speaks again, softer but no less commanding. "You can come out now. Fluffy is gone, and you'd best explain yourselves before he's back. I'm not in the mood for sneaky types."

As he steps into the clearing, Vaelior signals to the others to stay behind him. The scene before them is as bizarre as it is unsettling.

A figure stands by the fire, leaning casually on a gnarled staff that seems more tree root than wood. She is an old woman, her grey hair wild and frizzed, spilling out from beneath a tattered scarf that looks like it has seen a few too many stormy nights. Her eyes are sharp, glinting like a predator's as they scan the group. Despite her age, she stands tall and straight, her posture authoritative.

At her feet, sprawled on the ground near the fire, is Digram. His small form is limp, his face pale but peaceful, as though he were merely asleep.

"Digram!" Beryl cries, rushing forwards, but Vaelior's hand shoots out to stop her.

"Easy," the elf warns, his gaze fixed on the woman. "We don't know her intent yet."

"Intent?" the woman scoffs, narrowing her eyes. "He's not dead if that's what you're worried about. Just a little ... shall we say, stunned? Fluffy has a habit of being overenthusiastic regarding new finds."

"And Fluffy is ... ?" Minelira asks

cautiously, her hand resting on the hilt of her sword.

"The most adorable companion one can wish for," the woman says matter-of-factly, gesturing towards the woods where the beast had disappeared. "Big, mean and annoyingly clingy. I found him when he was an abandoned pup. Don't let the orcs fool you. Those brutes may ride his kind, but the beasts aren't as dumb as their usual riders. Fluffy has a mind of his own, and he thinks I'm his pack leader."

"More like his chef," Beryl growls, glancing at the fire and then at Digram.

The woman shrugs. "A bit of both, perhaps. But I'm not a killer; I'm a healer, I promise you that. I cook more potions than soups, if you want to know."

"We do," Lady Minelira says. "What kind of healer?"

"One who minds her own business . . .

mostly. You can have your halfling back."

Beryl bristles. "If he's harmed, so help me, I'll—"

"He's fine," the woman interrupts, waving her hand dismissively. "But you'd better take him and go before Fluffy returns. He's not as forgiving as I am."

Beryl rushes to her husband and takes his face into her hands. "Wake up, Diggie."

"A healer?" Minelira squints suspiciously. "The one who gave helpful advice to the cave troll?"

"Which one? Silly? Is that what he told you?" The old woman shrugs again. "Well, I suppose he could have. He is that sort of troll."

"Was." Vaelior steps forwards. "And what of you? What's your stake in all this?"

The woman smirks. "My stake? I live here, elf. These woods are mine. There are no walking trees here in the Forest of Noon-Fogs. I am not interested in your adventures, squabbles or precious halfling. But if you're wise, you'll heed my warning. This forest is no place for wanderers at night."

"And why's that?" Minelira asks, her voice steady despite the tension in the air.

The old woman's smile widens. "Because there are things out here far worse than Fluffy. With magic more powerful than mine."

"And they might be?"

"My wicked sisters. . . In law."

Digram's eyes snap open as if he had never been unconscious.

"What did you say?" he demands, sitting up abruptly and rubbing his head. "We were looking for you! You . . . and your, uh, soup." His voice wavers as his gaze flicks nervously to the bubbling pot over the fire.

"You were pretending to be unconscious this whole time?" Beryl scowls, grabbing and pulling him to his feet with no effort. "By the rocks, Diggie! I was worried sick!"

"Well, technically, I was unconscious — briefly," Digram admits, brushing off his waistcoat with exaggerated dignity. "But, you know, a little extra affection is worth the extension. Then I heard something about 'wicked sisters' and thought it best to join the conversation."

The old woman cackles. "A funny one, aren't you? But tell me, halfling, why are my sisters so important?"

"Because they are part of the song," Digram answers, puffing up slightly. He raises a finger for emphasis. "No, no. Do let me finish, esteemed mistress—"

"Breezewort," the old woman says, her grin widening.

"Yes ... Mistress Breezewort," Digram says, bowing theatrically. "I hope my friends won't mind if I tell you how this journey started and why."

Digram turns to his companions.

"Sure, you do it better," says Beryl with a huff. "Just don't waffle."

"Someone has to," Lady Minelira quips.

Lord Vaelior merely shrugs.

And so the halfling Digram begins to recount what should have been at the start of this tale but could not be, for I didn't know it myself until now. Let us hear his story, in his own words, of what happened just a few weeks before this starry night.

9: The Leaky Barrel

The tavern is not so much a building as it is a suggestion of shelter. A low, sprawling structure leaning precariously against the roots of an ancient oak, it seems to stand by the sheer will of its patrons. The sign swinging over the crooked door reads *The Leaky Barrel*, though it might just as well be called *The Splintering Table* or *The Dubious Brew*. Inside, the air is warm with the smell of fresh pies, wet dogs and the faintest hint of despair.

By the fireplace, a beautiful woman sits alone, dark curls falling over her shoulders as she sips from a tankard and reads a small tattered book. Around her, the noise of drunken chatter ebbs and flows like a tide, and is punctuated by occasional bursts of raucous laughter.

One particularly ambitious man, sporting a moustache so large it deserves a seat of its own, stumbles over, emboldened by equal parts ale and his companions' jeers. After a few false starts, he manages to plant an elbow on the mantelpiece, striking what he likely thinks is a roguish pose.

"What's a commoner like you doing in such an exquisite place as this?" he slurs, flashing a grin that probably works better in his imagination.

"Waiting for her husband," the woman replies without glancing up from her page.

"Well, why wait alone?" the man presses, his voice teetering on the edge of sincerity and sleaze. "He's let you down, hasn't he? You look sad. Let me cheer you up."

The words are met with laughter from his friends, who raise their mugs in mock applause.

The woman remains calm until the man is emboldened further, then reaches for her book. That is when her tankard and his moustache collide with a satisfying clang, sending ale flying in every direction. In the stunned silence that follows, she stands, seizes the man's arm, and twists it in a way that suggests she is intimately familiar with all the angles it shouldn't bend.

The door creaks open, and a smooth voice breaks the tension. "Sorry, my love. I'm late."

The moustached man, still grimacing in pain, hisses, "No, no, mate, you're just in time."

The woman releases him, and he scuttles back to his friends, clutching his arm and muttering under his breath. The other patrons quickly return to their drinks as if such incidents were as common as spilled ale.

The lady turns, her fierce expression softening as she wraps her arms around the tall figure who has entered. The elf leans down to kiss her. His light hair mingles with her dark curls as they exchange quiet words.

Before their reunion can continue, the door slams again.

A stout dwarf with a mane of silky curls and rosy cheeks stomps in, her axe resting casually on her broad shoulder. She inhales deeply, her face lighting up. "Ah, now this is a proper place to gather one's thoughts," she declares.

"It smells like it's already gathered everyone else's thoughts and left them to ferment," mutters the halfling, who trails behind her, his nose wrinkling.

"It's not about the smell," the dwarf says, striding confidently towards the couple by the fireplace. "It's about the ambience. The promise of ale, bad decisions and at least one good fight before the night's done."

"You do know we're here to plan, not fight, don't you, Beryl?" the elf says, ducking to avoid the wooden beams. "Though my lady already had a taste of one before I arrived to prevent it."

Meanwhile, Digram has already clambered onto a chair twice his size. He surveys the room with the eye of someone who has seen many taverns, and lived to regret half of them. "I like it," he declares. "Solid chairs, uneven tables. Plenty of character. And look at that barmaid! She's got more gaps in her smile than my cousin Bennor. Admit it, Vaelior, you can't fake authenticity like that."

A wiry barmaid appears at their table, her scowl as sharp as her elbows. Without so much as asking, she slams down four tankards of ale. "What'll it be?"

"Four bowls of potato stew, venison pies, and pickled pears," the dark-haired lady says, setting her book aside and taking her seat.

"I hope this is your finest ale," Beryl says, slapping a coin on the table. "And by finest, I mean something that won't dissolve the bottom of the mug."

"You're in the wrong place for that," the barmaid replies, snatching the coin and stomping off.

Vaelior sighs, settling onto the edge of his chair with the caution of someone expecting it to collapse. "We are here on the promise of a grand adventure," he says, exasperated. "And this is where we choose to plan it? A tavern?" He glances at the dark-haired woman. "Minelira, my love, surely there are better options."

"Better here than on an empty stomach," Digram interjects, grabbing one of the mugs. He sniffs it, winces and takes a tentative sip. "Besides, every great quest starts in a tavern. Ask any bard worth their lute."

Minelira raises an eyebrow. "How many of those bards survive long enough to finish their tales?"

"Survival's overrated," Beryl says, grinning as she raises her mug. "Now, drink up, all of you. We'll need our strength for what's ahead. Diggie, tell them."

The halfling puffs out his chest, preparing to speak. All eyes turn to him, and he grins, knowing this is his moment.

I don't know about you, my precious readers. Perhaps your ears are younger and more expedient than mine, but I cannot quite hear what brave Digram is whispering to his companions. They fall into what might be called a companionable silence, or at least the closest thing to it when dwarves, elves, halflings and humans share a table. The fire in the hearth crackles, throwing a warm, flickering light over their faces, while the hum of drunken voices and clinking tankards forms the backdrop, one of tavern life. Let us lean in closer, shall we? Here . . . now do you hear him?

". . . And since their power dwindled with time, like the last dregs of a candle, no one even wonders what became of them. All odd numbers. But the question is — where is five?"

The barmaid brings food. They wait for her to leave and dine in silence for some time.

Vaelior leans forwards, his face shadowed by the flickering firelight. His voice drops low as though the weight of his words might break something delicate if spoken too loudly. "Do we really need to bother with magic rings? Even if five magic rings exist, their power, like the others, is long gone."

"And why," Minelira asks, setting her mug down with a soft thud, "do you believe they were ever made? I've never heard of them. Have you, my love?" She glances at Vaelior, her expression curious.

"No," he replies. "And since my kin usually forged magic artefacts, I would know of five if they were real. Someone — anyone — would have mentioned them."

"Yet they did," Digram mutters, almost too quiet for the others to hear. His fingers tap the rim of his mug, his face unusually serious. "You've all heard the song. Everyone knows the famous words . . . or thinks they do. But the last lines are always left out. Forgotten. Deliberately, perhaps. Yet I know them from the old journal of one of my ancestors, who was . . . let's say, more than involved in those events."

Beryl's eyes narrow as she fixes him with a stern glare. "Don't you dare sing it here, Diggie," she warns, her voice a low growl. "Not in this place. Someone might hear you."

Digram hesitates, his mouth opening and closing as though battling between his love of singing and caution. He doesn't sing, but his voice drops to a conspiratorial whisper, his words barely audible over the tavern's hustle and bustle. The last lines appeared to be heard by everyone:

> . . . *Five for the wicked sisters and brother*
> *Bound by deceit to betray one another.*

Despite the whispers, these words hang in the air like the echo of a bell tolling in the distance. The fire in the hearth flickers once, then goes out entirely, leaving their table bathed in shadow. Around them, conversations falter. The usual raucous tavern sounds seem to drain away, leaving only a heavy, uneasy quiet. Even the light from the lanterns seems dimmer as if the tavern has drawn a sharp, collective breath.

Digram's companions sit frozen, their faces lit only by the faint glow of a solitary candle on the table.

"You just had to say it out loud, didn't you?" Beryl hisses.

"I didn't think it would—" Digram begins, but Minelira silences him with a quick gesture.

Vaelior's sharp eyes scan the room, his elven senses attuned to the change. "Something is wrong," he says softly, his tone clipped.

The other patrons seem to sense it, too. A nervous murmur ripples through the crowd, but no one looks directly at their table. It is as if some unseen force has passed through the room, pressing on their chests and making the air heavier and harder to breathe.

The wiry barmaid appears from the shadows near the bar, her scowl deeper than ever. Her voice cuts through the tension like a blade. "You lot should finish your drinks and leave," she says, her tone flat yet edged with something like fear.

Digram swallows hard. "Well," he says, attempting to sound casual. "That's one way to clear a room."

But no one laughs.

In the darkest corner of the tavern, a figure wrapped in a cloak sits motionless. Our heroes don't notice it, but I swear it wasn't there before.

10: Mistress Breezewort

Lord Vaelior declares the witch's soup "delicious." This is high praise coming from an elf.

Digram, however, eyes the wooden bowl with suspicion. "Vegetarian soup," he mutters, "might be good for the body, but it leaves the soul crying for a sausage."

Yet even he, after much sighing and mumbling, scrapes the bottom clean, leaving not so much as a drop, and asks for more.

After carefully considering their story, Mistress Breezewort decides to help them for her own reasons. She sits by the fire while the recently returned Fluffy curls up next to her after a very slobbery introduction to the party.

"As you know, I am a healer," she begins.

"And not a bad cook," Digram offers, apparently unable to help himself.

"*Not bad* at many things," Mistress Breezewort shoots back, fixing him with a sharp look. "But do interrupt me again, shorty, and I'll make a stew out of you next."

Beryl chuckles into her spoon; the others pretend not to smile.

The healer speaks again, her face serious. "Now listen. As I was trying to say, there are five rings forged by an elf maddened with grief and whose body was broken by orcs, and whose skill was exploited by one greedy mage."

At this, all four companions put down their spoons. Even Digram.

"Oh, we are listening."

"I will tell you everything. So . . . I might be a healer and a decent witch, but my ex-husband, unlike me, was not too good at wizardry. Not for lack of talent but because he had no patience to build his craft. Always in a hurry for the next shortcut. Once, he exploited a craftsman with incredible skills and a destroyed soul. That was the start of the trouble. My husband thought he had found the way to be the greatest wizard of all, but he lacked the wisdom to understand that real power is not in how big the mountain you manage to move is, but in knowing the reason for doing that. Not why, but what for."

She pauses, her eyes half closed. "Nevertheless, the old mage had enough wits to simply retire instead of causing more trouble with his experiments. We didn't get along, as I was a constant reminder that he was a failure. So he went to the other end of the forest to his sisters, three old maids. Before they wore the rings, the three wise women were called witches only because they understood a bit about the weather and how animals are born. There, my husband found a new calling and, for several hundred years now, has been the keeper of the five rings. This calling turned out to be a curse, consuming him so much that he can no longer think of anything else and does not even remember his own name these days, let alone what life was like before this cursed burden."

Vaelior leans forwards, his voice soft. "What became of the elf?"

Mistress Breezewort's face darkens. "They say his grief consumed him. He is no more."

"So you know everything about the rings?" Beryl prompts, clearly unimpressed with this detour into domestic history. "Where are they?"

"I'm getting there!" snaps Mistress Breezewort. "You lot have the patience of pond skaters. Where was I? Ah, yes. The rings. All magical objects have a nasty habit of clinging. They whisper to you, twisting your mind like the roots of an old oak. But perhaps these five are the most powerful and dangerous because they fulfil the most secret desires. What could be more devastating for us all than if someone's wish came true? Think about it for a moment longer."

The companions sit still, their soup forgotten, their expressions ranging from unease to outright dread.

Minelira starts, "But ... if they grant wishes, surely they could be used for good. If the kind person—"

Mistress Breezewort rises, her expression darkening as she turns to her. "Stupid girl! Do you think they would listen to your babble about healing all wounds and the disappearance of all diseases? They do not care for your prayers. No. They dig deeper into the shadows of your soul. Into the corners you don't even know exist and would be horrified by. And they will grant those wishes whether you want it or not. And you are not a witch, and you will not be able to eliminate the consequences of at least some of your efforts."

The healer calms down, but she does not appear angry with Minelira, rather, some personal bitter experience is involved here. The old woman sits again and thinks while the others finish their soup. On her face, worn out by the years, both pain and sadness become visible; each wrinkle is like a line in a long and sad story that no one would want to read so as not to spoil the day. The silence is so vast that it feels as if even the night birds and the fire logs are humbled by her words.

Finally, Beryl speaks in a gruff but kind tone. "You've seen this, haven't you?"

Mistress Breezewort's eyes meet hers, and for a moment, there's a flicker of passion. "Aye.

I've seen it. And if I had my way, those rings would be buried so deep not even a dragon could find them. But it's not up to me, and it's not the way. How long have you been on the road?"

"Almost eight days," Beryl answers.

The old woman nods. "Yes, yes. Then it all fits together. That's when he summoned me and started mumbling some nonsense about visitors coming soon. He had a vision of himself sitting in a tavern. He summoned you too."

"But why does your husband *want* us to find the rings?" Vaelior asks.

"To get rid of them, of course," the healer says. "Did I forget to mention that? The poor man has only one wish left. He wishes to be free of their magic. And that's why you're here, but he feared the sisters would want to stop you. He did something to them. I have not felt their power for the whole week." Breezewort sighs.

"Magra, Disara and Sletka are complex characters. Do not be put off by appearances. Sletka is not as attractive as she might seem, Disara is not so authoritative, and Magra is not as grumpy as she might look. It's just her resting witch face. If you find them and help them, they will help you. They know what must be done to unmake the rings. And remember," she adds, glancing at Digram, who is the closest to her huge pet, "appearances are deceiving. A beast might look harmless, fluffy even—"

"Fluffy is harmless," Digram says indignantly, scratching the ear of the enormous, slobbering animal.

Mistress Breezewort raises an eyebrow. "Is he now?"

Fluffy yawns, revealing a set of teeth that could crush bone with the ease of a chef slicing bread. A pool of saliva grows under his mighty jaws. He is really just as fluffy as your grandfather's leg.

The companions exchange uneasy glances, the weight of their task settling heavily on their shoulders. Somewhere, hidden in shadow and fire, the rings wait. And so do the secrets that will change the fate of their world.

11: Fight, Fight, Fight!

They sleep the rest of the night by the healer's fire, lulled into an unlikely peace by a curious combination of factors: the soporific herbs Mistress Breezewort tosses into the flames, the satisfaction of full bellies, and the reassuring presence of Fluffy, whose determination to guard their slumber at any cost is clear in his tiny eyes. It is, perhaps, the sort of peace that only comes when one is too tired to remember all the reasons one should be afraid.

As for me, I have my own reason for being confident in Mistress Breezewort. Without prompts, she heals Lady Minelira's blisters and fixes her limp. The girl shouldn't suffer for the rest of this story, and perhaps she will choose more sensible shoes for her next hike.

Though its efforts are somewhat half-hearted, the sun has already scaled the heavens when they awaken. The sky above is a muddled canvas of fog, clouds and possibly smoke, casting a pearly, diffused glow that suggests the sun might have been up all night playing cards with the moon and lost.

After a breakfast of bacon and mushrooms — it looks like Fluffy somehow managed to find a wild pig during the night — they prepare to leave. The healer hands Vaelior a peculiar object, a shard of pottery etched with odd markings that seem to squirm if you look at them for too long.

"Smash this on ... well, you'll know when and on what," Mistress Breezewort says cryptically, as though clarity might spoil the moment.

And with that, they set off.

Fluffy trots alongside them for a time, his tail wagging like a pendulum of enthusiasm. He whines happily whenever Digram calls him a "good boy." Eventually, the great beast turns back towards his mistress to resume his role as chief snorer of the healer's camp.

The road winds upwards for a while, birches with their yellowing leaves flanking the path like sentinels. The grass is brittle underfoot, already showing the wear of impending winter. It is Minelira who breaks the silence, her voice tinged with unease.

"For some reason, it feels like we spend not a single night but several months underground in the tunnels of stone moles. Look at the trees. Their leaves have turned, and the grass is dying. Yet it was summer when we started."

"It's the Forest of Noon-Fogs's altitude,"

Beryl replies with the confidence of someone who has spent more time than she'd like trudging through mountainous terrain. "We're climbing higher into the foothills. Up here, it's always a step away from winter. Witches love grim places like this."

"I can't shake the feeling that we're being sent to our doom," mutters Digram.

"Relax, my overly cautious friend," Vaelior says with a faint smirk. "If the esteemed Mistress Breezewort wanted to betray us, we wouldn't have woken up this morning."

"That's not what I meant," Digram grumbles. "I mean, there's trouble ahead."

"Of course, there's trouble ahead." Vaelior laughs. "We're looking for witches whose magic could incinerate us faster than a dry leaf in dragon fire."

As the day wears on, the road grows rougher and the air heavier, tinged with the faint smell of decay. The sun begins its descent, and they stand at the edge of a vast, murky swamp. The water stretches out before them in sluggish rivulets, choked with reeds and draped with curtains of mist.

Minelira wrinkles her nose. "This must be it. The swamp Mistress Breezewort mentioned."

"It smells like home," Digram says scornfully.

But something is wrong. The swamp is not as quiet as swamps tend to be — a fact made evident by the guttural barking of orders and the faint clang of metal on metal. Vaelior raises a hand to halt the group, his sharp eyes narrowing. Beyond the mist, movement can be seen: figures hunched and broad, their armour crude but effective, patrolling with purpose.

"Orcs," he mutters.

Beryl unslings her axe. "Looks like the witches have already rolled out the welcome mat."

"Well, that's one way to keep visitors out," Digram quips.

"Quiet," Vaelior says, hissing, his hand resting on the hilt of his blade. "We'll need to find a way around — or through. But one thing's clear: our goal is well guarded."

Our heroes have no time to decide their next move, for the foul blare of a horn shatters the swamp's heavy stillness, announcing their presence to all who lurk within its murky bounds. From the crude huts scattered across the waterlogged terrain, orcs burst forth, brandishing grotesque clubs and snarling with a feral rage. But they are not the only threat.

What appear to be harmless grass tussocks suddenly shift and twist, revealing hidden forms as the orcs shed their cunning disguises. Clumps of vegetation and mud fall away from their bodies, exposing wiry limbs and jagged armour. Even the swamp itself seems to come to life as hulking figures rise from beneath the stagnant water, dark forms emerging from the sludgy nightmares given flesh. The orcs tower to their full height, dripping with muck and menace, their pale eyes gleaming with malice.

Vaelior is already in motion, his bow in hand, an arrow nocked and drawn with practised ease. The string sings its deadly tune as his gaze sweeps over the advancing horde, searching for the first target in what promises to be a battle as grim and unrelenting as the Noon-Fogs itself.

The swamp erupts into chaos. Orcs pour from every direction. The guttural wail of the horn is a herald of chaos, and it galvanises both sides into action.

The elf's hands work with impossible speed, nocking arrows and releasing them in a blur. Each shot finds its mark — a glint of steel through an orc's throat, a shaft burying itself in a screaming foe's chest. His movements are fluid, a dancer weaving death into the fabric of the battlefield.

Beryl is no less magnificent, her axe a whirlwind of destruction. She wades into the fray like a storm, her every swing cleaving through armour, flesh and bone with terrifying efficiency. An orc lunges at her, a wicked blade raised high, but Beryl catches the strike on the haft of her weapon, twisting with a feral grin to bury the axe deep into the creature's skull.

Minelira, her sword gleaming even in the dim swamp light, fights with the poise of an experienced knight. Her strikes are precise, her parries effortless. She ducks low to avoid a swinging club, the tip of her blade slashing out to sever her opponent's hamstring before rising with a flourish to deliver a killing blow. "You have no manners! How rude!" she mutters, already turning to face her next foe.

Even Digram, the halfling who often prefers to stay out of harm's way, surprises them all. He moves like a shadow, darting between orcs with uncanny speed, his small size making him a difficult target. Daggers gleam in his hands, and with every throw, an orc falls, clutching at a throat or a pierced eye. "Didn't think I had it in me, did you?" he shouts breathlessly, a manic grin plastered across his face.

The orcs press harder, their numbers seeming endless. But for every brute that steps forwards, another falls. The swamp becomes a graveyard, littered with bodies sinking slowly into the muck.

Soon, our brave warriors notice that the ranks of the orcs have thinned considerably. First, one orc throws down his crude weapon and bolts, darting like a startled hare between the trees, clearly resolving never to return to these cursed parts. Then another breaks ranks and another. Within moments, the battle is over. The last orc stands frozen, his large ears twitching, his bulging eyes wide with disbelief. His ferocious war cry wavers, falters and finally dissolves into a high-pitched wail of terror.

He runs.

"They have no leader!" Vaelior shouts, nocking another arrow to his bow.

The shaft flies true, pinning one of the fleeing orc's floppy ears to a birch tree. The creature shrieks in pain, flailing as he attempts to free himself, but Vaelior is already upon him. The elf's hand shoots out, gripping the orc by the throat as soon as the creature decides to sacrifice his impaled ear to escape.

"If you talk, I'll let you go," Vaelior says, his voice calm, though his breath comes quicker than usual.

The orc flails in his grasp, black blood dripping from the torn ear. After a few panicked kicks, the creature wheezes and croaks, "What . . . do you . . . want?"

Vaelior loosens his grip slightly, only to flip the orc upside down and seize him by the ankle. The unfortunate creature dangles helplessly, his terrified gaze meeting Beryl's steely eyes.

"Speak," Beryl growls, resting a hand on the hilt of her axe. "Or I'll chop you up like cabbage for pickling."

The orc gulps. "The witches! The witches brought us here from the desert ...threw us into a storm! Only this swamp's mud stopped us from crashing to bits when we fell. But they . . . they never said why!"

"Until today," Vaelior prompts. "What did they say today?"

The orc squirms. "Only one thing. 'They're coming, they're coming.' So we thought that's why we were here ...to stop whoever *they* are. Then . . . then you arrived."

"And where are these witches now?" Vaelior demands, his tone sharp.

"In the very centre of the quagmire," the orc croaks.

Vaelior releases his grip, wiping his hand on the hem of his tunic. The orc falls unceremoniously into the muck. He scrambles to his feet, staggering a few steps as if to flee again, but then clutches his chest with a gurgle and collapses, unmoving.

"Did he just die from a stroke?" Beryl asks, raising her bushy brows.

"Where is Minelira?" Vaelior interjects, his voice taut with worry.

"Here," comes a faint voice.

They spin towards the sound to find Lady

Minelira half buried beneath a heap of orc corpses. The three rush to her side, freeing her from the grisly mound. After a quick inspection, it seems none of them have sustained more than minor bruises and scratches.

"I'd wager the healer had a hand in this luck, my love," Vaelior says, purring affectionately and brushing a mud smear from Minelira's shoulder. But before she can reply, a sudden cry of anguish pierces the swampy air.

"My backpack!" Digram wails. "Where's my backpack? Has anyone seen it? It has all our bacon!"

Beryl turns to him, exhaling with relief. "Stop this, Diggie. We need to find the witches."

Digram slumps, his face a mask of despair. "Forget the witches," he moans. "This is the real tragedy."

12: Three Wicked Sisters

Can the air pressure truly change in a particular part of the forest, under the open sky, merely because you and I approach a quagmire enchanted by a failed magician? I can't say for certain. But my ears feel blocked, and the air seems thick and unwilling to be breathed. Yet, look! It appears our heroes remain impervious to such atmospheric oddities, for they stride forwards and stop in bewilderment at the edge of the treacherously smooth, bright green surface.

In the centre of the quagmire, hovering perilously close to the water, are three figures, suspended as if some cruel puppeteer has left them dangling mid-performance. Their postures scream indignation, arms frozen mid-gesture as though hurling curses at the world. Only their eyes move, following every step of the approaching heroes, and their mouths twist in snarls.

The witches — because who else could they be? — wear similar threadbare dresses, their hems frayed from too many close calls with thorns and muck. Rough shoes adorn their feet, and sackcloth cloaks are draped over their shoulders. They look like sisters, hideous and ancient but not entirely devoid of unique quirks. One has long-faded flowers tangled in her white hair, while the other two, with their hair pulled into tight buns beneath faded scarves, differ mainly in height and girth.

The tallest, with a back as straight as a mast and bony shoulders, breaks the silence. "Have you come to mock old women in their misfortunes?"

"Not at all," Minelira replies, her voice measured. "We've come seeking help and advice. Instead, we were greeted by a pack of orcs claiming you summoned them to attack us."

"A blunder, I can't deny it," admits the shortest of the three, her doughy face pale and folded like uncooked pastry. "But you're here to kill our brother, aren't you? At his own call and folly."

"Perhaps at his call," Vaelior replies, his tone cautious, "but only to fulfil his wish. We seek the rings. The healer on the other side of the forest told us it is his will to pass them on, so he might finally rest."

"Ah, Breezewort and her infernal meddling," hisses the witch with the flower-strewn hair.

"Be quiet, Sletka," barks the bony one, her voice sharp as snapped twigs. She can't turn her head, only squinting fiercely at her sister. "Believe me, elf, we've had time enough to ponder my brother's last wish. For hundreds of years, I thought family was the cornerstone of all things. We had to protect one another, even as the rest of the world was swallowed by dragons or burned to ash by the rulers of men. But in all those long years, I failed to see what had become so painfully clear while hanging over this foul water. It is not my place to decide what is best for my brother. I may be the eldest, but the days when I carried him in my arms and changed his swaddling clothes passed so long ago that countless generations of mortals have lived and died since."

"Well . . . if not for you, Magra, it finally dawned on me! I would have married in my time and borne nephews for you. But no, you forced me to take up the craft of witches, which was never mine by choice," mutters Sletka, glaring as though the statement has been building up for centuries.

"Silence, Sletka," snaps her sister Disara. "That groom of yours was a scoundrel, and Magra had nothing but good intentions."

Digram interjects before the argument can spiral into ancient grievances, raising his hands like a man trying to calm a stampeding goat herd. "Ladies! With respect, your family squabbles are fascinating, but we're here to help each other, aren't we? Mistress Breezewort said you knew how to rid the world of these rings. And I, for one, think that's a good idea."

Magra, her gaze icy, flicks her eyes to the left. "We'll not tell you anything while we hang here like wet laundry. Find the pedestal over there. Our brother may be a fool, but he knows a thing or two about runes."

Beryl approaches the brambles, shields the pedestal and hacks through the brambles with her axe. Beneath the tangle of thorns lies a weathered stone column, ancient as the hills, its runes glowing with eerie, recent magic.

Minelira leans towards Vaelior and whispers, "You know what to do, don't you?"

The elf draws the clay shard from within his tunic, his expression unreadable.

"Wait, wait!" cries Digram, waving his arms as he turns to the witches. "Forgive my impertinence, mademoiselles, but your reputation is ... let's say, colourful. If your intentions are truly noble and your honour unblemished, swear to us now that you won't deceive us. Let there be no trickery. Promise that you'll provide us aid and support. And that your brother will receive peace."

The three witches all roll their eyes, a synchronised gesture full of weariness.

"Well, that's on us, I suppose," Disara admits with a reluctant shrug. "There was probably no real need to confuse the local villagers."

Magra, still grim-faced, agrees. "Fine. We swear to do all we can to help you."

"And after we say farewell to our brother, we'll go back to Breezewort and take up our old lives," Sletka chimes in.

"We'll deliver babies — human and bovine alike — and we'll predict thunderstorms and make poultices for blisters, ointments for rashes and cough remedies," Disara finishes matter-of-factly.

"Good enough for me," Beryl declares, stepping back.

Vaelior slams the shard into the pedestal with all his strength. Instead of shattering, it vanishes like the stone has swallowed it whole. The runes on the column flare in a blinding light and then fade away.

Behind them comes a deafening splash,

followed by sputtering and indignant cries.

The witches, finally claimed by gravity, fall from their suspension into the swamp. Their tangled cloaks and skirts become soaked and weighed down with muck and duckweed. They climb to the dry grass and scramble to their feet with surprising vigour, swiping at each other.

"I want to give him a slap or two like in the old days!" grumbles Magra, brushing a particularly stubborn lump of algae from her shoulder as though it were some high-born insult.

"Filthy water!" cried Sletka, clawing at the remains of the swamp slime clinging to her hair. But as her fingers pass through the tangled strands, the hair darkens, transforming into a cascade of long red locks. The faded flowers entwined in her hair blossom, their colours as vibrant as a midsummer meadow. Her once-wrinkled face gains a youthful glow, powdered with freckles.

"Diggie, I have never seen glamour in action before," whispers Beryl in Digram's ear.

"I am sure we see it daily. We just don't know it," the halfling answers, watching the transformation like a show.

Disara, meanwhile, hauls herself upright with a grunt. She is now a rotund woman, her cheeks round and ruddy, her skin fresh with the vigour of someone who spends much of their time bossing people about. She scrubs furiously at her sleeves, the damp fabric clinging to her large arms.

Magra stands tall and unmoving, brushing away stray duckweed with a frown of indifference. Her angular face remains severe, untouched by the transformation that has affected her sisters. Yet her tattered dress shimmers as if infused with starlight, reshaping into a flowing gown of velvet blacker than the void of the night sky. The subtle glint of silver embroidery traces constellations across the fabric, adding an almost regal majesty to her already-commanding presence.

"Typical," Sletka mutters, eyeing her now-perfect sister. "She barely gets her feet wet while we're up to our necks in muck."

"Because I don't thrash about like a frantic goose," Magra retorts. Her voice is as calm and sharp as a winter wind, her cold eyes narrowing. "And because I have dignity. You should try it sometime."

"Enough, both of you!" Disara snaps, wiping her hands on her dry apron, which has appeared out of nowhere. She turns her sharp gaze to the adventurers. "Now let's get on with it."

Minelira tilts her head, taking in their new appearances. "I see no reason to doubt you," she says.

"Good," says Magra, crossing her arms and glancing at the pedestal. "Because there's much to be done, and I'd rather not waste time convincing you that we mean no harm. What's next is your part of the bargain."

"Bacon would be nice," Digram mutters, shaking swamp muck from his boots.

Vaelior steps forwards, his voice steady. "Tell us how to defeat the rings and take us to your brother."

The witches exchange looks, their eyes speaking of decades — perhaps centuries — of unspoken understanding. Finally, Magra inclines her head and the group braces themselves for the truth.

What they learn chills them to the core. The five rings were never meant to be remembered. Some of this they had gleaned from the healer; the rings granted their bearers what they desired most.

But, dear readers, consider this: not what one might idly fancy over tea on a sunny afternoon, but what lies buried deep within. The truest, most desperate wish forged in moments of rage, grief or despair. As you know, that can be the most terrible thing of all.

The witches knew this better than anyone. They had once worn the rings themselves long ago. Wicked though they became, they were not fools. They dared not wear the rings again or allow them to fall into mortal hands. Instead, they passed the burden to their brother.

Their brother, a victim of his own errors, was the least likely to covet the rings' power. His only wish, unwavering for centuries, had been simple: to keep the rings safe. And so, the rings had granted his wish, twisting his existence into something otherworldly. They bound him between time and space, between life and death.

Over time, even this simple wish began to

waver. His almost spectral existence became a torment. Above all else, he wished to die and be free of his commitment. But the rings resisted as if sensing their own doom in his death. They kept his mind clouded and him trapped, unable to die truly, too weary to live.

Finally, in his desperation and rare moment of sanity, he made one last wish: for anyone to come and free him. The rings responded, probably happy to grant a wish that might ensure their chance to return to the world. The mage sensed the faintest mention of the rings in a faraway town from his desolate swamp. And so, he waited.

"For decades, he has lingered," Magra says, her voice low. "Waiting for someone brave – or foolish – enough to answer his call. A few days ago, that happened."

"To free our brother and abolish the rings, they must be forgotten," Disara adds, her tone grave.

"Forgotten?" Minelira echoes, her brow furrowing.

"Yes," Sletka says, her dark hair gleaming in the faint light. "Their power is bound to memory and desire. The moment they are forgotten, their grip will weaken. But as long as they are remembered, they will persist."

Digram frowns, shifting uneasily. "But how can something be forgotten unless we all lose our minds in unison?"

"We don't know," Disara replies. "Even our brother failed to want it enough, with the absolute purity that the wish required."

Magra nods solemnly. "We love our brother, no matter what. We don't want him to die. But we cannot bear to see him suffer for eternity either."

Her words hung heavy in the air, mingling with the damp chill of the swamp.

13: Brother

I have a difficult task, dear readers: to describe to you the hapless mage, brother to the three witches and former husband of Mistress Breezewort. But I shall endeavour to try.

Picture a nameless man who is both present and absent, a contradiction wrapped in frailty. You see him once, but if you glance away, even for a heartbeat, he seems to dissolve into the shadows. No, he is not transparent, like a ghost or flat, like a reflection or a painted image. Yet, as you stand before him and look into his eyes, an eerie sensation creeps over you – a certainty that you are entirely, irrevocably alone.

How do I do? Hmm, not well, I fear. Apologies, dear reader. Some things are beyond words, and the Old Man is one of them.

The witches keep their promise, leading our weary band through a winding mountain gorge to their lair. It is a fortress of wood and stone, as impenetrable as the witches' secrets. Yet, somehow, it also manages to be a brewery, copper boilers steaming and pipes humming, overlaid with the charm of an ancient workshop where old magic still lingers.

The witches stay above ground while our heroes descend into the heart of the lair. Countless stairs spiral into the cold depths, every step echoing with a sense of finality. At last, they reach the bottom – a place older than the mountains, more frigid than death, and silent as an unspoken prayer.

At its centre, seated on the bare earth, is the Old Man.

He is more a shadow of a person than a man – a frail, fuzzy figure draped in tattered robes weighed down with trinkets and baubles of witchcraft. His body is thin, almost weightless, and his frame is hunched beneath an unseen weight.

His bony fingers bear five rings. Initially, these rings were crafted with exquisite skill. But now, they are blackened and cracked, as if the very spells they hold have corroded them from within. Their dark power gnaws at his flesh like rust on iron.

His pale, hollow eyes seem to peer into a distant void far from this world. His voice is little more than a rasping whisper when he speaks, like dry leaves dragged across stone by an unforgiving wind.

And so, the heroes behold the tragic figure of the mage, the brother who has borne the curse of the rings for centuries.

"You seek the five," he says. "At last. I bear them, and they bear me—"

The four friends freeze. The Old Man lifts trembling hands, the rings shimmering faintly as though resisting him even now. "Power cannot be shattered – it can only pass on. I wait for five who can shoulder the burden. And now . . ." His hollow gaze falls upon them as though seeing through to their very souls. ". . . five stand before me."

Digram coughs, rubbing his chin. "Old man, there are only four of us."

The silence is heavy. Vaelior shifts uneasily, Minelira's face unreadable, and Beryl frowns.

"No," the Old Man whispers, his cracked lips curling into a shadow of a smile. "There are five."

Everyone turns to Minelira. Vaelior's expression shifts. "Minelira . . . are you—"

"What? No! I'm just tired. I'm a human, a race not so gifted as your lot. Despite the training."

Digram, however, gasps, spinning towards his wife. "Beryl?"

Beryl groans, muttering dwarven curses. "Yes, Digram Oldbook. I'm expecting."

The halfling lets out an excited squeak. "I'm going to be a father?" He seizes Beryl in a clumsy hug, nearly knocking her over.

"Pull yourself together, Diggie," Beryl mutters as her cheeks flush. "It's not the first half breed in the world, although it might be a slightly improved one."

The Old Man wheezes a tired sigh. "Then it is done. The burden of five will pass – through the living, through the new. You ... are enough."

He stretches his hands towards them, and as though pulled by unseen strings, each companion plucks a ring from his withered fingers. Beryl hesitates, then takes two.

"What do we do now?" Vaelior says, holding the ring with two fingers as if it might bite him. "I don't trust myself to wear it. I am an elf, and my deepest desires are unknown even to me, buried deep in the ancient legacy of my race."

"And I'm at the other end," Digram says, shrugging. "I live for today and might accidentally wish for a pie the size of a barn."

"Human whims can't be trusted," Minelira adds, her voice soft but firm. "But I would always trust a good mother. A mother can't wish for anything bad for her child."

Beryl looks at her friends, the slight fear of responsibility creeping into her expression.

"My lady isn't wrong," Vaelior says. "If anyone can be trusted to truly wish for the rings to be forgotten, it's you, Beryl."

"I . . . I . . . suppose so." Beryl's eyes flick to each of them, uncertainty clear.

"Here, darling, let me help you with a song," Digram says softly. He squeezes Beryl's hand, his voice steady but tender as he begins to sing:

> *You might say you wish for a bunch*
> *of flowers,*
>
> *But deep in your heart, you're*
> *craving lovers.*
>
> *You might claim you long for a tale*
> *to be told,*
>
> *But truly, you're itching to speak*
> *and be bold.*
>
> *You might think you're building a*
> *house of stone,*
>
> *Yet dream of a town where your*
> *name will be known.*
>
> *You might wish for treasure, all*
> *gleaming and grand,*
>
> *But you'd trade it for armies at your*
> *command.*

You might cry for peace on a clear,
quiet night,

But deep down, you're wishing to
see foes in flight.

Yet when you whisper, "Safe, let
my baby remain,"

No masks, no deceit – just a hope
free of stain.

For gold may bring power, and
songs may deceive,

But a heart that loves truly has
nothing to grieve.

Beryl closes her eyes, tears slipping down her cheeks. With the final line, her hands stop trembling. She slips one ring onto her finger. She does not say a word, but at that moment, everyone knows – she wants to forget about those dangerous rings more than anything.

All five rings slowly begin to fade, dissolving into thin air as the Old Man releases a final, shuddering breath. His face softens, and the invisible weight that has burdened him seems to lift.

"You have chosen well," he murmurs, although it is unclear to whom he is addressing those words, barely audible, before crumbling to ash.

14: The Epilogue

Ah, dear readers, I trust you've been well in my absence! And what of our heroes, you ask? What have they been up to in the last couple of years? Well, come closer, and I'll show you. Behold – a scene to warm even the coldest of hearts!

Today the companions gather in Digram's snug little home. The halfling cradles a sleeping baby, its tiny curls peeking from beneath a soft blanket, while Beryl sits beside him, looking both proud and slightly smug.

Minelira and Vaelior watch them, their smiles warm and gentle.

"So, this is —" Vaelior starts softly, his voice filled with affection.

"A girl!" Beryl replies with a smile.

"Nice! And I hope her beard will be as glorious as her mother's," Minelira chuckles.

Digram grins down at the child. "We've named her Pearl," he says. "After Beryl's favourite aunt. I did suggest Digramma, though I'll never know why she vetoed it."

"Because it's ridiculous," Beryl snaps, but her smile betrays her affection. "Pearl Oldbook sounds better."

Vaelior places a large ribboned box onto the growing pile of gifts. "I must be getting old, Beryl. I don't even remember why we had to travel all the way to the edge of the Noon-Fogs just to fetch a batch of herbal potions for you from a healer."

"It was a dangerous journey, my lord," Minelira replies with a shy smile. "Plus, now it turns out to be not just for Beryl, but for me too." Vaelior stares at her for a moment. Then, the realisation dawns, and his face softens as he leans forwards, pressing his lips to her hand with closed eyes.

The fire crackles in the hearth, casting a golden glow across the room. Digram's voice is soft, almost a whisper, as he speaks half to the child, half to the night.

Three birds will circle high in the sky,
To mark your road as they glide and fly.
Seven stones will steady your feet,
Each step is a promise, firm and sweet.
Nine friends will stand, strong and true,
Through shadowed night or morning's dew.
And five great deeds, bold and clever,
Will carve your name to live forever.

As Pearl stirs in her sleep, her small eyelids flutter open. A strange, bright light gleams from her eyes for a brief moment.

But perhaps it is simply the fire's reflection.

The end.

Thank you for finishing this book. The author would greatly appreciate an honest review if you're willing. Thank you again

And now — the teaser.
Coming soon: *The Forgotten Five* **is followed by**
a new game, *The Curse of the Half-Breeds.*

Here's your first look — the official trailer:

Pearl was the first to push herself up, coughing soot and brushing ash from her hair.

"Well, that went swimmingly," she spat, glaring at the smoking crater where goblins had been seconds ago.

Beside her, the purple-skinned tiefling halfbreed groaned, horns scraping stone as he rolled onto his side. "You lit the fuse too soon, Pearl. I barely cast my shield.

"It wasn't me!" Pearl shot back. "That was one of their fire pots, not mine."

"But it was you who—"

The dragonborn woman let out a low growl, flames licking her teeth as she tested her scorched gauntlet. "Enough, Dorivey. Blaming each other won't mend wounds."

"You are right, baby. Come and give me a kiss of life," Dorivey said, now on his back, his voice sounding as if each word cost him.

"I will give you a slap if you do not get off my tail. Now!"

Then came a rattling cough. The rogue lay sprawled where he'd landed, unnaturally still. His long ears twitched once, then he sat up, grimacing.

"Dead gods," Octosias muttered, spitting blood into the dirt. "Do I look like a bomb sponge to you lot?"

For a moment, silence. Then Pearl laughed — sharp and tired. "You do now."

Her laughter cut short when she noticed something in the dust. She stooped, dragging up a severed goblin forearm. The hand still clenched a jagged blade, skin inked with crude black letters. The words curved halfway round the stump, stopping mid-phrase: *The property of the curse-lifter Jerto…*

Pearl's brow furrowed. "That's no tavern

mark. It's a slave brand."

Xaithra leaned closer, nostrils flaring. "Half a sentence." She scanned the blackened corpses. "Where is the rest of it?"

After a short search among the dead, both hacked and whole, Octosias narrowed his eyes, wiping grime from his chin. "Looks like the rest is out there... attached to the goblin that ran."

Dorivey managed a crooked grin. "Well then. We chase him."

Pearl tightened her grip on the severed arm. "No argument here. We find him, finish the line and maybe find his master, who will break this curse for good."

Dear reader, I wish they would hurry. All my senses are insulted by what's left here, and I feel sick. Plus, it is raining again. The fight was over, but the force binding them together only tightened. I will follow them, if only to learn what they'll do next.

THANK YOU

MORE BY THIS AUTHOR:

Sci-fi series:

- ACT & VIST (- 1) short prequel 2024
- OBJECT & VIST (1) 2021
- CONSTRUCT & VIST (2) 2022
- VIST & PROPER GANDA (3) 2023
- WHO WAS VIST (4) 2024
- WHEN PLATIMUN RUSTS (1) 2025
- WHEN PLATINUM RURSTS (2) 2026

Gamelit Fantasy novellas:

LEVELLING UP TOGETHER:
- THE FORGOTTEN FIVE (1) 2025
- THE CURSE OF THE HALF-BREEDS (2) 2026
- THE PRICE FOR DOING RIGHT (3) 2027

Part in Anthology:
- 2024 Next Generation Short Story Awards Anthology of Winners
- Borne in the Blood (WolfSinger Publications)
- The Dragon's Hoard 2 (WolfSinger Publications)

\-

ABOUT THE AUTHOR

Anka B. Troitsky, a multi-award-winning author and philosopher, came to the UK in 1993. With a rich background as a science teacher, translator of books, Law and NHS interpreter, she channels her diverse experiences and insights into the science fiction and fantasy genre, exploring the depths of what she has learned and understood throughout her journey.

You are welcome to Subscribe for an Email list:

www.ankatroitsky.com